"You low-down skunk!"

A female voice denounced coldly. "How dare you still be asleep!"

Brody rubbed his eyes, still too groggy to take offense. What a way to start the day! The caller continued her colorful, nonstop verbal invectives.

"Do you hear me?" she asked.

"It'd be a little hard not to, lady. Half of Oklahoma County can hear you. Who is this, anyway?"

"You know who it is! Do you have any idea how disappointed your two little sons are right this minute?"

Sons? "Now wait just a darn second—" Brody began.

"I'm through waiting. I want you to get your butt out of bed and meet us in front of the zoo's gorilla compound in one hour. If you're not there, don't you dare ever close your eyes again!" With that ominous threat, the mystery caller slammed down the phone.

Brody sighed. He tried to get back to sleep, but the voice of the woman on the phone haunted him. Trouble was, he had no idea *who* she was . . . and he didn't have any sons!

Dear Reader,

When I think of the month of June, I summon up images of warm spring days with the promise of summer, joyous weddings and, of course, the romance that gets the man of your dreams to the point where he can celebrate Father's Day.

And that's what June 1990 is all about here at Silhouette Romance. Our DIAMOND JUBILEE is in full swing, and this month features *Cimarron Knight*, by Pepper Adams—the first book in Pepper's *Cimarron Stories* trilogy. Hero Brody Sawyer gets the shock of his life when he meets up with delightful Noelle Chandler. Then in July, don't miss *Borrowed Baby*, by Marie Ferrarella. Brooding loner Griffin Foster is in for a surprise when he finds that his sister has left him with a little bundle of joy!

The DIAMOND JUBILEE—Silhouette Romance's tenth anniversary celebration—is our way of saying thanks to you, our readers. To symbolize the timelessness of love, as well as the modern gift of the tenth anniversary, we're presenting readers with a DIAMOND JUBILEE Silhouette Romance title each month, penned by one of your favorite Silhouette Romance authors. In the coming months, many of your favorite writers, including Lucy Gordon, Dixie Browning, Phyllis Halldorson and Annette Broadrick, are writing DIAMOND JUBILEE titles especially for you.

And that's not all! There are six books a month from Silhouette Romance—stories by wonderful authors who time and time again bring home the magic of love. During our jubilee year, each book is special and written with romance in mind. June brings you *Fearless Father*, by Terry Essig, as well as *A Season for Homecoming*, the first book in Laurie Paige's duo, *Homeward Bound*. And much-loved Diana Palmer has some special treats in store in the months ahead.

I hope you'll enjoy this book and all the stories to come. Come home to romance—Silhouette Romance—for always!

Sincerely,

Tara Hughes Gavin
Senior Editor

PEPPER ADAMS

Cimarron
Knight

CIMARRON
STORIES

Silhouette *Romance*

Published by Silhouette Books New York

America's Publisher of Contemporary Romance

This book is gratefully dedicated to
Jack and Wynona Brooks.
May you always grace the Winner's Circle.

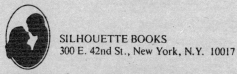

SILHOUETTE BOOKS
300 E. 42nd St., New York, N.Y. 10017

ISBN: 0-373-08724-1

First Silhouette Books printing June 1990

Printed in the U.S.A.

PEPPER ADAMS

lives in Oklahoma with her husband and children. Her interest in romance writing began with obsessive reading and was followed by writing courses, where she learned the craft. She longs for the discipline of the "rigid schedule" all the how-to books exhort writers to maintain, but does not seriously believe she will achieve one in this lifetime. She finds she works best if she remembers to take her writing, and not herself, seriously.

A Note From the Author:

Dear Readers,

I am thrilled and excited to participate in Silhouette's DIAMOND JUBILEE celebration. For ten years, Silhouette Romance has brought you some very special love stories, unmatched in quality and excellence. The editors consistently recognize the important reader-author link and the Silhouette Romances offered this anniversary year reflect that commitment.

As a native Oklahoman, I enjoyed writing about my state, the Quarter Horse Capital of the World. My trilogy, *Cimarron Stories*, evolved out of a desire to share the excitement I experienced while researching the spirited racing industry. Relatives in the business provided a number of excellent, firsthand resources.

In *Cimarron Knight*, a wrong number tempts horse trainer Brody Sawyer to keep a rendezvous at the zoo, where he meets Noelle Chandler. The pretty divorcée and her towheaded twins are destined to steal his heart.

Coming in September is *Cimarron Glory*, in which Brody's foster sister, Glory Roberts, returns home to begin her practice in equine medicine. And while she's at it, maybe show Ross Forbes, the ornery cuss who spurned her childhood affections, that she's all grown-up now and ready for love.

Cimarron Rebel, featuring Brody's younger brother, Riley, is just the ticket for warming up those cold November nights. Riley's marriage of convenience to pert country-western singer, Darcy Durant, becomes a matter of inconvenience when they find it impossible to keep their hands-off bargain.

Thank you for making me a part of the Silhouette Romance tradition.

Sincerely,

Pepper Adams

Chapter One

The insistent jangle of the telephone dragged Brody Sawyer from the sweet oblivion of exhausted sleep. The ringing registered somewhere in his muddled mind, but he couldn't rouse his bone-tired body enough to make it stop.

Instead, he buried his head under the pillow and hoped that whoever was creating the disturbance would do so again later. Much later, when he was better equipped to deal with it.

But the caller was not so obliging and the ringing persisted. When he had rallied enough to lunge for the receiver, Brody grumbled into the mouthpiece, his gravel-edged voice sounding even hoarser than usual, "Yeah?"

"You low-down skunk," a female voice denounced coldly. "How dare you sleep? You thoughtless, selfish jerk!"

"Huh?" Brody rubbed his eyes, still too groggy to take offense. What a way to start the day—get cussed-out first thing in the morning and nothing worse could happen all day. Normally, he didn't inspire such anger in women and he racked his tired brain for a clue as to this one's identity.

The caller continued her colorful, nonstop verbal directives until Brody's ears hurt. And he'd thought he'd heard it all before.

"Do you hear me?" she demanded.

Brody tried to recall what woman, if any, he might have riled to such bitter invective. "It'd be a little hard not to, lady, half of Oklahoma County can hear you. Who is this, anyway?"

"You know good and well who it is, you sorry, good-for-nothing SOB. How dare you break your promise. Again!"

That comment was Brody's first clue that the lady was doing her barking in the wrong woods. Adhering to a policy he'd made early in life, he did not make, much less break, promises. He gave his solemn word in business dealings but scrupulously avoided the kind of empty, hurtful promises that had scarred not only his childhood but that of his younger brother Riley.

"I've had it this time, buster," the woman said in a tightly controlled voice. "Do you have any idea how disappointed your two little sons are right this minute? Do you?"

Sons? "Now wait just a darn minute—" Brody began. She clearly had the wrong so-and-so, but she didn't give him a chance to point that out.

"Wait? That's a good one." Her laugh was mocking and Brody knew she wasn't smiling. "The boys and I have done nothing but wait. And for what?"

"Well, I—"

"Don't bother to answer. For once in your worthless, disappointing life, don't talk at all. Just listen. It's bad enough that you won't support your own children. Any self-respecting man with a shred of decency would do that much. But what I find totally reprehensible is that you're too selfish and lazy to make an effort to see them regularly. Is that asking too much?"

"Lady..."

"I said don't talk."

Brody smiled. She was on a roll. He could have ended the whole tirade by hanging up, but he didn't. In spite of his efforts to remain detached, he was becoming intrigued by the little melodrama unfolding courtesy of Ma Bell.

"Are you listening to me?"

"Yes, ma'am, I..."

"I said don't talk. I want you to get your butt out of that bed and haul it over to the zoo like you promised Dusty and Danny. We'll meet you in front of the gorilla compound in one hour. If you're not there, don't you dare ever sleep again, you slime, because I will not be held responsible for what might happen to you if you do."

With that ominous threat, the mystery caller slammed down the phone and Brody took the full angry force of it in the ear. Bewildered, he dropped the receiver and collapsed back on his pillow. "Crazy woman," he mumbled.

After a quick glance at the luminous digits on the bedside clock, Brody saw that it was ten-thirty. He'd had less than two hours' sleep after spending the night walking a colicky horse. It had been long after sunup, when he was sure the valuable animal was out of danger, before he'd turned its care over to one of his men.

Bright Oklahoma sunshine, too hot for the first day of May, blazed outside, but Brody was in no mood to appreciate the gifts of nature. He fully intended to go back to sleep and forget the entire episode, which had to be the worst case of wrong numberitis he'd ever heard of.

But as hard as he tried he could not get back to sleep. The trembly outraged voice of the woman on the phone haunted him. Her voice sounded like one that wasn't often raised in anger, even when anger was justified. Despite her creativity, the woman had seemed uncomfortable with the expletives. He wasn't accustomed to such displays of raw emotion, but he'd recognized held-back tears in her words.

He wondered if she'd given into them once she slammed down the phone. Was she now crying inconsolably with no one to comfort her but the two little boys who'd been watching out the window for a neglectful father who never showed up? He found himself trying to conjure up a picture of the woman's face.

Brody punched his pillow. Since when did he have so much imagination? And since when were an unknown woman's tears and unknown children's disappointment any of his business? Maybe it wasn't fair that they'd been stood up, but when he was a kid a whole army of half-forgotten social workers had taken professional pride in pointing out that life wasn't always fair.

Naw, disappointment wasn't fatal. He and Riley were living proof of that.

For all he knew the woman could have bled her ex-husband dry in the divorce, just as his former sister-in-law had tapped out Riley. Riley was at home right now, sleeping off a bender and no good to anyone including himself. He'd never been much of a drinker before Candi had stripped him of all his possessions. Now he'd lost everything from liquid assets to self-respect.

Too generous for his own good, Riley had given the woman what she wanted. Brody had contributed his fair share, too, mortgaging Cimarron in the process. They'd done it for the children, but Candi still wasn't satisfied. Now she was giving Riley a hard time about seeing his stepchildren. She wouldn't be happy until he was completely broken and tossed aside as if he were a misused horse.

That wouldn't happen—not if Brody had anything to do with it. He'd vowed to save his brother from his self-destructive ways or die trying. That task could prove both difficult and thankless. Brody was as hardheaded as Riley.

When Brody closed his eyes, he thought of those little boys again, Dusty and Danny she'd called them. He compared them to the two raggedy unwanted brats he and Riley had been. Yeah, he knew what it was like to have a father who went back on his word. Damn, that was the trouble with promises—they were too quickly made, too easily broken.

Brody rolled onto his stomach and pulled the pillow over his head. The darkened room was silent except for the gentle whirring of the ceiling fan. He'd installed one in every room to rid the house of institutional air. He traveled a lot, running the horses he trained for others in races around the country. Of all the disadvantages of motel living, Brody thought inhaling "recycled" air was the worst.

It wasn't long before Brody figured out that he wasn't going back to sleep, though why he wasn't sure. He reminded himself that the faceless, nameless woman's problems were none of his business. Why couldn't he just forget her call had ever happened?

He lay in the rumpled bed a few more minutes before throwing back the covers. Not knowing exactly what he was going to do, he got up and dressed in a pair of worn blue jeans and a pale blue Western shirt.

Sitting on the bed to pull on his boots, Brody cursed his shred of humanitarianism that refused to let the mother and kids think they'd been stood up again. He'd have to make the rendezvous at the zoo and explain.

It was a dumb waste of time, but then again, most good deeds were. Maybe he could prevent unnecessary mayhem. After all, even a low-down skunk, child-support dodger deserved better than to die in his sleep.

Jaunting off to the zoo was the last thing he needed to do, but Brody went to look for his top hand to let him know he'd be out of pocket for a while. He crossed the well-tended yard and called a greeting to Bobber Smith, an old wrangler who wouldn't retire. He seemed content to putter around in the flower beds and Brody kept him on the payroll because he was a friend.

Brody stepped into the cool interior of the main barn, a grand structure that never failed to impress him. It was enormous, streamlined and modern. Everything in it was state-of-the-art. Cimarron Training Stables had earned the enviable reputation of being one of the best quarter horse training facilities on the circuit. It was Brody's goal to make it the undisputed best.

He'd worked hard to get where he was, mainly because of Dub Roberts. Everything Brody was, he owed to his foster father. Dub and his wife Ruby had taken in the scruffy Sawyer boys when the system gave up on them. Their real parents had provided little more than a tenuous start in life, but the Roberts had given them love, stability and self-respect.

He'd worked unnecessarily hard to earn Dub's ready approval. Brody knew nothing of horses when he arrived at Phoenix Farms, but he'd learned fast. At ten he was an apprentice stable-swamper; at twenty, a savvy trainer. Thanks to Dub he now had his own place where he boarded and trained the hobby horses of the wealthy.

He'd been lucky. The horses he trained placed in the money more often than not, and his services were in demand. Each day brought him closer to the realization of his dream.

But Brody never took his success for granted. He put most of his money back into his operation. He wasn't seduced by the trappings of the good life and lived simply most of the time. His one weakness was first-class air fares. When a man logged as many miles as he did that little bit of luxury went a long way.

He was known as a "good boss" and wranglers vied for positions on his payroll. His men were loyal and dependable and kept things running smoothly in his absence. Like Riley, Brody was a little too generous and the only person he never cut any slack for was himself.

Horse owners—primarily doctors, lawyers, athletes, and others with more money than they could spend—trusted him to protect their investments. They respected him because he respected their animals and had an innate ability to find and develop a horse's full potential—a highly profitable skill, both for Cimarron Stables and its clients.

Brody found Billy Sixkiller in the sick horse's stall. "How's he doing? I have to go out for a while, but I'll stay if you need me."

"You go on, Boss. This one'll be okay."

The Cherokee had forgotten more about horses than Brody ever hoped to learn. "I'll take your word for it, Billy. If you said he'd fly, I'd start looking for wings." Brody dropped his pager into the pocket of his denim jacket, just in case.

"So what're you waitin' for, Boss?"

"An excuse not to go, I guess." He ran an experienced hand over the animal's belly.

"Where you headed?"

"The zoo."

"The zoo?"

"That's right. You got a problem with that?"

"Not me. You're the boss."

"Now, why do I get the feeling you're just humoring me?" He strode out the door and heard Billy chuckle behind him. What did he find funny?—the idea of having a boss or the notion that Brody was gallivanting off to the zoo on what was sure to be a wild-goose chase?

Chapter Two

In time-honored Oklahoma tradition, Noelle Chandler was fit to be tied. The animosity she'd felt toward her ex-husband when she talked to him on the phone had not dissipated one bit during the twenty-minute drive from her house near Penn Square to the Oklahoma City Zoo.

It was a good thing her four-year-old twins, Dustin and Daniel, were so engrossed by the gorillas' antics or they would have been frightened by the intensity of her rarely displayed temper.

"This is the last straw," she muttered through clenched teeth as she paced the area. She'd checked her watch all too often and knew exactly what time it was. Ten more minutes. That's all she'd give him. If Steve didn't show, she'd forget he was the boys' father and let her lawyer, Eve Franklin, have her way.

Eve was primed and ready to file suit against Steve for eighteen months of unpaid child support. That was not very responsible of him, considering they'd only been divorced two years.

New child-support-enforcement laws were high on the state legislative agenda. More attorneys and judges recognized the problems nonsupport by financially capable fathers placed on the family, as well as on the state's economy. Eve assured her Steve could be jailed for contempt of court for not making court-ordered payments.

Normally Noelle wasn't a vindictive person. Hadn't she given Steve more second chances than she could now count? But he had a responsibility to the boys and if he wouldn't discharge it by at least keeping the promises he made, she'd have him in jail before God could get the news. A few weeks behind bars would adjust his attitude and make him wish he'd found a little more time in his "busy" schedule.

"Lookit the baby, Momma," Dusty squealed. He was on his knees looking through the barrier at the gorillas in the big grassy enclosure below.

"Lookit the big one, Momma." Danny wasn't about to let his brother have the last word. "Is he the daddy?"

"I think so, sweetie." Down below a big silverback scooped up an infant and cradled it gently in his powerful arms. An alert female sat nearby eating an orange while two juveniles romped on a tire swing. They presented the very picture of domestic gorilla bliss, which was more than some human families could do.

Noelle's glance lingered on her lookalike towheads and her mood softened. Poor babies. It wasn't fair that their father was such a louse. All Dusty and Danny wanted was a daddy—someone to depend on, to look up to, a father they could respect and love and model their own lives after. Instead they had the irresponsible, emotionally-stunted Steven Chandler, who didn't possess the paternal instincts of a gorilla.

Brody approached the gorilla observation deck warily. He'd had time to think about what he was going to say when he encountered the woman on the phone and he still hadn't come up with anything sensible. He'd just have to wing it. Or go home.

Then he saw her. A little blonde, with twins to match, was checking her watch and scanning the Sunday morning crowd. When she didn't spot the person she was searching for, her bright blue eyes took on a desperate, murderous look.

No doubt about it, Brody wouldn't want to be in her ex's boots when she finally caught up with him. The lady looked fit to be boiled down for glue. Maybe he should forget the whole thing and leave. Let her figure out her mistake on her own.

He retreated a few steps, then turned for another look. She was talking to the boys now, as though trying to distract them from noticing that their father hadn't shown up yet. As much as Brody wanted to, something wouldn't let him walk away. Maybe it was the proud tilt of her chin, or the vulnerability and hurt in her wide-set eyes. Hurt, he knew inexplicably, that she did not deserve.

He liked the graceful way her small, compact body moved despite her agitation and distress. She didn't look like the kind of woman who would bleed any man dry. She looked soft and sweet and gentle. She laughed at something one of her boys said and her face was transmuted with beauty that bubbled up from inside her.

She glanced around again, anxiously this time, and Brody experienced a primitive urge to punch the man who'd put the sadness in her eyes.

Against all good sense, he was drawn to the woman, his latent protective instincts activated against his will. Before he knew what he was doing he stepped up to her, doffing his hat like Ruby had taught him to do when in the presence of a lady.

"Good mornin,' ma'am. My name's Brody Sawyer and I believe we talked a while ago." He fired off one of his disarming grins and thrust out his hand.

Noelle was startled when the tall cowboy spoke to her and instinctively gathered the boys closer. It took her a moment to answer because a zoo outing was the last place she'd expected to be hit on. Warily she said, "Not a bad line. Must be a variation of the old standard, 'Haven't we met somewhere before?'"

Brody winced. It was downright discouraging that even when he was being sincere he didn't sound it. "No, really. You did call me this morning. About ten-thirty?" He winked and smiled mischievously. "Reach out and cuss someone?"

The lady looked confused and upon closer inspection, Brody thought she was even more fetching, her full lips formed into a polite but wary smile. He looked into her incredibly blue eyes and suddenly felt as if he'd been horse-kicked. "You had the wrong number," he said softly. "But it was me you asked to meet you by the gorilla compound."

And here he was. Noelle groaned when she recalled the general drift of the one-sided conversation. "Oh, no!"

"Oh, yeah." Brody grinned to show her he didn't bear any grudges. "Except it wasn't me you wanted to ask, was it? I believe you were extending the invite to some sorry worthless good-for-nothing thoughtless skunk-jerk SOB slime."

"My ex-husband." Noelle felt the heat rise in her face and cursed her fair skin that turned as red as chilblained hands when she was embarrassed.

"That's what I figured. You didn't give me a chance to slip a word in edgeways before you hung up, so I came here to..." Funny, he couldn't think of a single good reason why he had come.

"To point out my error?" she supplied with a half-hearted grin.

"Yep." Yep? Had he really said yep like a refugee from an old Gary Cooper movie? Where was suave when he needed it? Where was debonair? Hell, where was literate?

Noelle grinned. Yep. He was a cowboy all right. "Thanks for going to so much trouble, Mr..."

"Brody."

"Mr. Brody."

"Not Mr. Brody," he clarified. "Brody Sawyer. Call me Brody."

She ignored his attempt at familiarity. "Believe it or not, Mr. Sawyer, that's the first mistake I ever made."

"I guess everybody's entitled to one." He looked at her intently and got horse-kicked all over again. He decided it would be ungenerous to point out at this crucial stage of their acquaintance the big mistake she'd obviously married.

Noelle was uncomfortable under the man's appraising look and wished she'd worn her baggy jeans and a bulky shirt. He seemed a little bit too appreciative of what he saw.

"I guess I should apologize for getting you out of bed." She realized it was a woefully inadequate thing to say to a man upon whom she'd rained every curse she'd ever read in books or heard in movies. But an apology was definitely in order. "I really am sorry."

Brody swallowed hard. He should be the one apologizing—for thinking about getting her *into* bed. "It could have happened to anyone. You were pretty upset when you dialed."

"Actually, I'd passed the upset stage. I was well into murderous by then." She wondered if he'd been sleeping off the effects of too much Saturday night fun. If he had, he'd recovered nicely. She extended her hand and introduced herself.

"Noelle? A Christmas baby, huh?" Another brilliant observation, Sawyer, Brody chided himself. He had a moment of regret when he released her hand and chided himself some more. He wasn't sure why he was still hanging around now that he'd done his duty. He had a sick horse to see to and a brother who was probably feeling even worse right about now.

"December twenty-fifth." The hand Noelle drew back felt warm from the stranger's touch.

Brody felt a tug on his jeans and looked down into the upturned face of one of the little boys. It was round and framed with silver-blond hair cut in a bowl shape. The child's big blue eyes were bright with curiosity.

"Hey, mister, will you hold me up so I can see the 'grillas better?"

"Me, too, me too," piped up his brother who had the same hair and features.

Brody knelt down on one knee, but the children still had to look up at him. "First things first. How am I supposed to tell you guys apart?"

The one who'd spoken first said matter-of-factly, "I'm Dusty and he's Danny," as though that explained everything. "We don't dress alike, so all you gotta do is 'member I'm wearin' a blue shirt and he's wearin' a red shirt.''

"That sounds simple enough. But what if the next time I see you, *he's* wearing a blue shirt and *you're* wearing a red shirt?"

Both boys shrugged and giggled. Noelle put in, "They are identical twins, but once you get to know them, it's easy to tell them apart."

He hoisted the children up, settling one on each of his wide shoulders. "Maybe for you, ma'am."

"Will you do me a favor, Mr. Sawyer?" she asked with a grin.

"If I can."

"Stop calling me 'ma'am.'"

"You got yourself a deal. Providing you stop calling me Mr. Sawyer."

Noelle watched as he turned his attention back to the boys who chattered on about the gorillas. This was their favorite part of the zoo and they always spent extra time laughing at the animals' antics. While Sawyer was otherwise occupied, Noelle sneaked a closer look at the man who gave every indication of sticking around.

His Western shirt stretched across broad shoulders that were strong enough to hold seventy-five pounds of squirming boys without effort. He had the work-toughened look of a dyed-in-the-wool outdoors type and it was obvious that his scuffed cowboy boots weren't reserved for dancing the two-step.

In true cowboy fashion, he wore his belt buckle big and his Stetson low. This guy didn't just dress the part. He lived it.

The boys slid down to the ground when Brody did a deep-knee bend. As he did so, Noelle couldn't help noticing how his muscled thighs, among other things, strained against his work-worn jeans in an earthy testament to his masculinity.

In fact, the entire blue jeans industry was missing out on a sure thing. With Brody Sawyer in their ads they'd sell a few trillion pairs of denims, for sure. Mostly to lonely women who'd long since given up on finding a knight in shining armor and would be perfectly happy to settle for one in tight jeans.

Despite his physical perfection, the man seemed to take his good looks for granted. Or maybe he wasn't aware of the effect his blatant virility had on women.

Ridiculous. Any man who looked that good knew it.

When she looked up Brody gave her a sidelong glance. The grin twitching at his lips let her know he was aware she'd been giving him the once-over. The raised brow and sly wink seemed to ask if she liked what she saw.

Something fluttered in her abdomen and she called it embarrassment. After all, she'd been caught in the act. But as his gaze traveled over her face and throat to linger on the swell of her breasts, Noelle grudgingly admitted the feeling she was experiencing was a little more primitive than chagrin.

Despite their unusual meeting, Brody felt Noelle's approval as her gaze raked him over. She was a pretty woman. Her honey-colored hair had an alluring, tumbled look that invited a man's hands, just as her pale smooth skin invited a man's touch. Her heartbreaking blue eyes were surrounded by long thick lashes and her lips were full and tempting, features that seemed too big for her fine, delicate face.

She didn't have the hard-bodied look of a female who could beat a guy at arm-wrestling, either. She had a shape built for loving; soft and curvy. Her breathing accelerated and her breasts rose and fell in a slight, but maddening fashion. When her nipples peaked against the thin fabric of her shirt, Brody succumbed to something hot and consuming. He took a step forward.

The cowboy held Noelle's gaze as he moved toward her, his almost-smile fading as he searched her eyes. Their breaths mingled, and her lips parted in wonder as she stared back into his hazel eyes. As crazy as it was she wanted him to follow through with whatever impulse had gripped him. When he didn't, she was both relieved and disappointed.

"Momma, I'm dyin' of thirst," Dusty complained.

"Me, too," Danny agreed.

Brody stepped back abruptly, wondering what would have happened if the child hadn't interrupted his runaway train of thought. He would have most likely gotten his face slapped for what he'd had in mind and he figured he owed the boy a drink for saving him the embarrassment.

Grabbing the boys' hands he headed for the nearest snack bar. "Come on, Momma," he tossed over his shoulder. "Let's get my pardners here a root beer."

The drink turned into lunch and while they finished off corndogs, fries and soft drinks, the boys proved the adage that if you want to know anything just ask a four-year-old.

Dusty paused to take a bite of his corndog and Danny rushed to fill the void. "And our neighbor Mr. Rupert tole us he'd give us five dollars if we could talk Momma into havin' a date with him."

Dusty made a face. "Yuck. We had dates once and we didn't like 'em 'cause of the pits. But we tole Momma what he said and she said she'd just a'soon have a bad perm as go out with that ole—"

"Dustin!" Noelle had known the day would come when she'd regret her sons' articulateness.

"I know it's a bad word, but I was only tellin' Brody what *you* said," Dusty protested innocently.

"I know, but I had to put a quarter in the swear jar. And so will you if you repeat it."

Brody chuckled. "She must have made a sizable deposit this mornin'."

Dusty looked up at him and grinned. "I'll say. We prob'ly gots enough in the jar for a real bacation by now."

"Yeah," Danny supplied. "Momma gets this many days off from the bank." He held up all his fingers and gave Brody the impression that if he'd had more he would have held them up, too.

Brody ruffled his hair. "Just how big is this jar, pardner?"

"This big." Danny held his arms wide.

In an effort to get his share of attention, Danny sidled up and patted Brody's shoulder. "You wanna go on bacation with us?"

Noelle quickly reneged Danny's invitation. "I'm sorry, but as my grandmother would have said, the boys have taken a shine to you. Four-year-olds embrace the *mi casa, su casa* philosophy. They don't always know what they're offering."

For good measure she reminded the boys, "There will only be the three of us on this vacation, remember?"

"We remember," they replied in solemn unison.

For reasons he didn't fully understand Brody was gratified to hear the errant ex-husband was definitely out of the picture.

Just then the open-air Safari Tram full of sightseers caught the boys' attention. "Can we ride, can we ride?"

Brody wasn't sure which one asked the question, but wanting to put smiles on their little faces again, he promised quickly before their mother could refuse. "Sure, but it's my treat. I think your momma has better things to do with her money."

Noelle was about to inform him that she only swore when under duress, but the boys never gave her the chance.

They boarded the tram, the four of them sitting on the bench seat with the little ones in the middle. Brody asked over their heads, "What bank do you work for?"

When she told him he nodded. "I bank at another branch." He studied her for a moment. "What do you do there? If you tell me you foreclose on widows and orphans, I'll quit trusting my instincts."

"I'm the assistant operations manager."

"Sorry, you don't look like the banker type to me. You don't have those sharp corporate edges."

"I didn't really plan to have a career in banking, or anything else for that matter. But when the oil industry went bust and my husband's business suffered, I took a job as a teller to help make ends meet."

"And by dint of conscientious hard work you clawed your way up through the rank and file, right?"

"Wrong. I got booted up the ladder despite my lack of career aspirations. By then I was divorced and needed the money."

Since Brody already knew about her ex-husband's lack of support, he only smiled in understanding.

As the ride progressed and the boys' excitement level increased, the adults had to give up the seats where the view was better. This rearrangement put Brody and Noelle side by side, but Brody didn't mind the arrangement at all.

He should have returned to the ranch a long time ago, but he just wasn't ready to end the unexpected and surprisingly good time he was having. Eighteen-hour days and seven-day work weeks didn't allow much time for fun and now that he was having some he wasn't about to call it quits.

Brody was impressed with the patient attention Noelle lavished on her children. Although rambunctious and high-spirited, the boys were well-mannered and much loved. He couldn't help comparing them to his brother's maladjusted stepchildren. Maybe divorce didn't have to result in screwed-up kids, after all.

Above all, Brody was impressed with Noelle. She definitely wasn't the kind of woman he usually went for. His taste normally ran to the good times/good sport sort. The kind who didn't expect too much or make too many demands. Since he liked to lay his cards on the table, any woman who was willing to take her chances with him had to be smart enough not to let her heart get involved.

That's why he was so uncomfortable with his attraction to Noelle. She was more the bed and breakfast and babies type. Probably had a whole houseful of tasteful things designed to tie a man down. She'd want the promises he couldn't give. She'd want guarantees. She'd expect a lot from a man—not that she didn't deserve it.

Poor kid just wasn't savvy enough to realize the danger she was in. The kindest thing he could do for her would be to part company before things went any further.

That would be the *right* thing to do, but for the first time in ages Brody was genuinely intrigued. He wanted to know more about her, to understand the depth and complexity that were so often missing in the women he met. Horse sense warned him that he was making a big mistake by prolonging the inevitable, and as Brody was a big believer in horse sense, he felt bad about ignoring it. So bad, in fact, that he slipped his arm over the back of the seat in hopes of finding some comfort.

Danny had appropriated Brody's Stetson and asked curiously, "Are you a real live cowboy, Brody?"

"Yep." It wasn't lack of eloquence that led him to his monosyllabic response but the desire to stay in character.

"Do you ride real live horses?" Dusty wanted to know.

"Sure, every day. That's what I do for a living. I'm a horse trainer."

"How big is a horse, anyway?" questioned Danny.

"Ever'body knows that." Dusty boasted. "They're r-e-a-l big."

"Thoroughbreds?" Noelle's curiosity was finally getting the best of her. So far, Brody had revealed very little of himself.

"Quarter horse racers."

She sighed. So much for Sawyer's SQ, or suitability quotient. Noelle and her friend Darcy Durant had a system for working out just how close to their respective dream men potential suitors came. Brody scored high in overall looks, sense of humor and intelligence but occupation wise he had just bottomed out.

She'd already had one man in her life with an uncertain future, she didn't need another. What Noelle wanted was a man who kept regular hours and brought home a paycheck every Friday. A man who wanted his wife to be a homemaker in the truest sense of the word. A man who wore button-down collars and drove a nice dependable car. A man who was predictable and stable, not one who mucked stables for a living.

Danny was doing his job by not allowing her to have too many consecutive thoughts and asked Brody the burning question. "Are you a dad?"

"No," he answered with a good-natured grin.

Dusty frowned. "Then are you a husbin?"

Brody chuckled, not entirely ignorant of where the conversation was leading. "No."

"Then what are you?" Dusty wanted to know.

"An innocent bystander?" he offered.

Noelle grinned and in an effort to distract his interrogators exclaimed, "Look, guys, zebras." It wasn't wise to let the boys spill too much more of their collective life story. Sawyer already knew more about her than she did about him.

As the tram rambled along Brody kept up a steady stream of conversation. Noelle didn't know what to make of the brash cowboy. She glanced at him, noting the half grin, the twinkle in his eyes, the shoved-back Stetson that gave him a mischievous devil-may-care look, and warning bells went off.

Here was a man who could break her heart if she let him, and she wasn't about to do that. She'd already played that scene, and she hadn't forgotten the pain.

They took in the sights and Brody treated them all to cotton candy. Afterward, even with the help of premoistened wipes, Noelle declared the twins hopeless. She reminded Brody of a mother quail with a covey of chicks when she began the difficult task of herding her sons toward the parking lot.

Once there Brody helped buckle the boys into their car seats, then walked around to the driver's side. Noelle cranked down the window of her station wagon and waited with mixed feelings for his next move.

"Thanks for coming, Brody. It was kind of you to be so good to the boys. They're not around many men and your attention meant a lot to them."

He leaned down and folded his forearms on the edge of the open window. He was glad there hadn't been many men in their lives, or in Noelle's if he was any judge. "How much did it mean to you, pretty lady?"

His question unnerved her. "More than I wanted it to," she admitted honestly.

"Yeah," he agreed with a lopsided grin. "This was almost the most fun I ever had with a wrong number." He reached through the window and squeezed her hand gently. "Take it easy. And be careful who you call next time. Not everybody's as easygoing as I am."

As he looked in the back seat, Brody admonished the boys, "You guys take care of your momma." They swore to do so.

And with that he tipped his hat and strode toward his dusty pickup truck.

Noelle hated herself for doing it, but she watched his well-shaped backside until it slid into the driver's seat. Then she shook her head, hoping she could shake his image out of her mind.

No doubt about it, she'd gotten off easy this time. A man like that was sure to be more than she could handle. No way should she even think about seeing him again. So why was she so disappointed that he hadn't asked for her phone number?

The chattering in the back seat reminded her of more immediate concerns. What was she thinking allowing herself to be swept away by a totally outrageous stranger? The man might seem like some kind of old-fashioned Western hero to two young boys starved for male attention, but he wasn't what she wanted in a man. Just because two four-year-olds had been impressed was no reason she had to be.

The attraction she felt was completely irrational in light of Brody's low SQ. She shouldn't even be thinking about him or the way he grinned or the way his muscles rippled. Any latent longings he'd aroused were academic anyway. He'd breezed in and out of her life like a tumbleweed, which was exactly how permanent a man like that would be.

She knew little more than his name and occupation, but that didn't stop her from speculating about how it might feel to be held in his strong arms. As dangerous as that kind of speculation could be, Noelle was painfully aware that Brody Sawyer, horse trainer, would occupy an annoyingly large portion of her thoughts tonight.

She wished she'd had the presence of mind to ask him a few questions, such as what had *really* motivated him to come here today. He'd been interesting and interested and obviously had a way with the ladies. So why hadn't he asked to see her again? Where was he going now? Was there a woman waiting for him?

She started the car and laughed wryly at the sheer magnitude of unanswered questions Brody inspired.

"Hey, guys?" she called to the giggly little boys in the back seat. "Who was that masked man, anyway?"

Chapter Three

Momma?" Dusty tugged at Noelle's skirt as she washed the dinner dishes that evening. "I'd sure like to have me a hat like Brody's."

"Me, too," Danny added with enthusiasm.

"Mr. Sawyer's," she corrected. "We'll keep that in mind for one of your birthday presents. Why don't you two go outside and play on the swing for a while?" The boys raced for the door, much to her relief.

Brody this, Brody that. It was beginning to get on her nerves. She wanted nothing more than to put Brody Sawyer out of her mind completely, but Dusty and Danny had made that impossible by chattering about him all afternoon. The tall cowboy had made a big impression on her very impressionable sons.

He's not really a cowboy, she amended. He was a horse trainer for Pete's sake. He trained horses to race. Races meant pari-mutuel betting and that meant gambling. He probably bet on the horses he handled, living in tall cotton when they won and on the edge of good-ol'-boy bumdom when they lost.

Noelle slung the dish towel down on the counter. Why was she always attracted to men who had an aversion to steady work? Easy Come, Easy Go was a financial motto she was unhappily familiar with.

If Steve weren't so unreliable she wouldn't have made that fateful phone call and she wouldn't be thinking about a man she had no business thinking about. She put away the last of the dishes and switched off the light. Too bad she couldn't extinguish thoughts of a certain cowboy so easily.

She knew it was silly, but when the telephone rang her heart kicked up before she could remind herself that it couldn't possibly be Brody. Her vague disappointment turned into full-fledged resentment when she heard Steven's voice.

"Hi, baby. It's me."

Baby? His tone grated on her nerves. For Steve, baby wasn't a term of endearment, it was an insult. He'd used it for years to make her feel useless and helpless and sadly lacking in ambition. He'd called her baby to undermine her confidence and to shore up his own bulletproof ego. Even when she'd been supporting the family almost single-handedly, he'd referred to it as income from her "little job." Baby? She wasn't anybody's baby. Not anymore.

"Me, who?" she demanded.

"Don't be that way, baby. I know you're ticked off at me about that zoo business, but something came up."

"Too bad it wasn't your zipper."

"You've got a sharp tongue, Noelle, and a cold heart."

"Thanks to you. You taught me well."

"Now, baby, don't get all pushed out of shape. I would've been there if I could've. You know that."

"Get on with it, Steve."

"On with what, baby?"

"With the excuse portion of the program. Then I can get back to doing something important."

Steve took her at her word, preferring a combination of begging, whining and sweet-talking, a method he had used of getting around her that had proved successful in the past.

But not this time. "Now that I know where you stand, let me explain my position," she said with a lack of emotion. "The boys deserve better than nonsupport and broken promises from their father. Today was your last chance, I'll be calling my lawyer tomorrow."

"Ah, Noelle, be reasonable. I'm working on a big deal right now."

"You should try working on something else for a change."

His voice took on a note of familiar hardness. "Listen here. How can I pay child support when I don't even have a job?"

"Looks like you'd better get one. Quick. I'm through being reasonable. I'm going for mean." With that she hung up on him and left the phone off the hook so she wouldn't be tempted to answer if he called back.

Noelle spent the rest of the evening watching *Sesame Street* videos and playing games with the twins. When they were tucked snugly into bed she read a few of their favorite stories.

They were still reluctant to let go of the excitement of the day and stalled as long as they could. She held on to her patience when they asked for their third drink of water and asked for divine guidance when they had to make yet one more trip to the bathroom. Prayers were lengthy, since they asked God to bless each and every character on *Sesame Street*.

Little by little, they calmed and when their heads finally touched the pillows they were almost instantly asleep. They looked so sweet and innocent and vulnerable lying there and Noelle hoped they wouldn't be scarred too badly by their parents' inability to live together.

She took a last lingering look at her sons from the doorway and whispered, "Good night, my babies."

Half asleep, Dusty flopped over and mumbled, "Oh, yes, God bless Brody, too."

"Yeah, Brody, too," Danny said drowsily.

She eased the door shut and sighed. Brody again. She hoped the boys wouldn't be too disappointed when he didn't show up in the future. She went straight to her room and got ready for bed. It was early, but maybe if she fell asleep she wouldn't have to think about him. She hadn't figured on him invading her dreams.

The next morning Noelle dropped Dusty and Danny off at the day-care center before driving to work. After so much time, she still felt a small pang when she left them. She'd read the research that reported the children of working moms showed increased independence and enhanced social skills, but she couldn't help thinking her place was really at home with them.

The pressures of single parenthood were overwhelming at times, but they were made worse by the knowledge that she was missing out on some very important time in her sons' lives. Time that she wouldn't have had to forfeit under the old-fashioned rules. Was she the last woman in America who did not want it all?

When she got to work she was careful to answer the ubiquitous "How was your weekend?" with a casual but noncommittal "Fine." She wasn't about to share the details of her strange zoo encounter with her co-workers, especially with her best friend.

Darcy Durant meant well, but customer service wasn't her true vocation. She sang country songs for fun and profit, and her burning passion was advising the love-lorn. The ebullient brunette was a self-appointed war correspondent in the battle of the sexes.

While Darcy didn't necessarily believe in marriage, she suffered from what Noelle called the "Noah Syndrome." She wasn't happy unless everybody went through life two by two. Better not to give her any encouragement. Noelle didn't need or require Darcy's matchmaking skills, especially where Brody Sawyer was concerned.

By Friday she had given up any hope of hearing from him. That afternoon when she stepped out of an officers' meeting and glanced across the bank lobby, she was shocked to see a cowboy sitting on her desk. Big hat, long legs, wide shoulders.

Brody. She experienced a momentary feminine flutter about her appearance and was glad she'd worn her red silk dress. It always made her feel less like a banker and more like a woman.

It was all she could do to disguise her pleasure at seeing him again as she made her way across the lobby that was decorated in tasteful tones of teal and peach. She walked slowly, taking her time to observe his effect on the other women in the bank. She noticed with amusement that his presence had drawn out all the female antennae within a fifty-foot radius.

The ever alert Darcy was positively quivering. She wondered if any woman could ever be completely secure with Brody as her significant other. Not likely. He was simply not programmed for putting the female mind at ease.

She assumed he was dressed for work; his outfit fit him just as a three-piece suit fit a banker. He had on a faded denim shirt, jeans that had long since been broken in, a hand-tooled leather belt and boots. When he saw her he stood and removed his hat and Noelle was sure she heard a collective feminine sigh rise from the ranks.

She leaned against her desk and looked up at him, delighted to think he'd remembered where she worked and cared enough to look her up. "This is a surprise. I certainly didn't expect to see you here."

He held up a handful of receipts and cash as proof that he was on a legitimate errand. "I usually bank at another branch, but I was in the neighborhood and decided to drop by."

"Still using those tired old lines, I see."

"Why not, they still work."

"Have you been here before? I'd be delighted to show you the facilities if you like. We're very proud of some of the innovations here." Wonderful, Noelle thought, now she sounded as though she were a marketing rep.

A slow grin spread over Brody's facial features and his eyes twinkled. "I didn't come here to tour the facilities. In fact, just watching you walk across that lobby was enough to make the trip worthwhile."

Darcy strolled by and placed a memo on Noelle's desk. She heard Brody's remark and once she was safely past him, turned and waved her hand in front of her chest, mouthing something that looked to Noelle like ''wooo weee.'' She was so distracted by Darcy that she almost missed Brody's next comment.

"I said before that you don't look like any bank executive I've ever seen." He shook his head and, still grinning, said, "But you sure do sound like one."

She returned the smile. "Old habits, and all that."

"Maybe I should find out more about the tour," he said suggestively, caressing her with his gaze. "Any chance we could get lost. Alone?"

She looked into his eyes and saw deviltry there. "Not a one."

"Too bad." He leaned closer and lowered his voice. "You have the biggest, bluest eyes I've ever seen."

Noelle didn't know how to respond to such blatant flattery; she'd never been subjected to it before. A silly flutter began low in her abdomen and she felt the heat rush to her face as he slowly, ever so slowly, leaned toward her lips.

Just inches away he asked, "Do you have plans for the evening?"

A ringing telephone jolted her into remembering where she was. She turned as crimson as her dress when she considered how many pairs of eyes were watching the exchange. She backed away, putting the width of her desk between them. "This evening?"

"Sure. We could go out to dinner, take in a movie, or... whatever."

His look left little doubt about which whatever he had in mind. He certainly knew how to murder the moment. "I'm sorry, Brody, but it's hard to get a sitter on such short notice," she said pointedly.

He shrugged as if to say "Hey, I tried" and scribbled his phone number on her message pad. He glanced around and, for the benefit of the employees who were trying hard not to let their eavesdropping show, said in a businesslike voice, "Let me know what happens, Ms. Chandler."

Noelle watched the pickup back out of the parking lot, then sat down at her desk. She reached for the piece of paper with his phone number on it, just in case, and saw Darcy's "memo." She turned it over and smiled when she saw the message scrawled in her friend's untidy hand. *Great buns*.

She'd barely finished reading the short note when Darcy grabbed her elbow and steered her toward the break room. She thumped a cup of coffee down in front of Noelle and pushed her into a chair. When she'd settled with a cup of her own, the barrage of questions began.

"Who was that hunk? Are there anymore like him at home? Where did you meet him? Why have you been holding out on me? Tell me everything and don't spare the details."

"Brody Sawyer. I don't know. The zoo. Because I was hoping to avoid this interrogation." Noelle sipped her coffee. "Does that cover it?"

"That's it?"

"That's it. Oh, yes, he's a horse trainer."

Darcy looked impressed. "A horse trainer?"

"According to him."

"What's that mean exactly?"

Noelle shrugged. "Beats me. I guess he rides horses around a track or something."

"Okay, so he's not a rocket scientist. The way he looks, who cares?"

Noelle gasped in mock astonishment. "Are you suggesting I should be interested in Brody Sawyer as a sex object?"

"He's about the sexiest object I've seen in a while," Darcy retorted. "So you met him at the zoo. The zoo?"

"The zoo."

"When?"

"Last Sunday."

"Did he have his kids with him?"

"No, Dusty and Danny asked him if he was a 'dad' or a 'husbin' and he claimed innocence."

"Well, of course he would. Unless he's a hard-core animal lover, I just can't imagine a man like that hanging out at the zoo for no good reason."

"Oh, he had a reason." Noelle's eyes lit up over the rim of her cup.

"Aha!" Darcy leaned forward and her manner was playfully menacing. "Details, *mein fraulein*, details."

Noelle explained the wrong-number-inspired meeting and just as she'd feared, her friend ate it up. She told Darcy about Brody's casual offer of a date and how she was planning to turn it down.

"You're crazy to let a gorgeous specimen like that off the hook so easily."

"Darcy, he didn't give me much notice. Who's going to watch the boys? Besides, I don't like the way he just took it for granted that I don't already have a date."

"Do you?"

"No, but it was still presumptuous of him."

"Men that scrumptious are often presumptuous." Darcy smiled at her own joke. "If I didn't have a gig tonight, I'd keep the kids myself."

"Thanks for the offer, but I don't think I'd better get involved with the brawny Mr. Sawyer."

"Why not? You don't go out enough. If you did, you'd know what a good deal you're passing up."

"I didn't know you were so superficial, Darcy. You know absolutely nothing about the man, but because he has passable looks, you're ready to place your best friend's fate in his hands."

Darcy shrugged. "It's just as easy to fall for a good-looking guy as it is a homely one. Then when he becomes totally useless, he can at least be decorative."

"I have no intention of falling for anyone. Besides, I don't think we'd have much in common, other than the fact that we both think he's pretty cute. His SQ's a little low."

"According to whose calculations? Those eyes and that sexy swagger alone would make up for minor character flaws and any overt narcissistic tendencies. You just haven't been on the dating circuit long enough to realize that men like him are as scarce as hen's teeth."

Noelle carried her cup to the sink. "It's been my experience that women who are always looking for a man have never had one on a permanent basis. I have, and I'm not."

Her friend didn't take the dig personally. "I still think you should try to find a sitter."

She was determined to end the conversation. "I think we should get back to work while we still have jobs."

Throughout the rest of the day, when she should have been otherwise occupied, Noelle's mind drifted back to Brody's offhand invitation. The more she thought about it the less she liked it. On top of everything else, she had to reprimand one of the tellers, so she was cranky and out of sorts when she called Brody just before closing.

It took a while for him to come on the line and judging from the background noise, he'd answered on a mobile phone in a barn somewhere. "Brody, this is Noelle."

"I know." What he didn't know was why she sounded so unhappy about it.

"I thought I should call and tell you I couldn't get a sitter." It wasn't exactly a lie. Maybe she hadn't tried, but she didn't have one all the same. "I guess I'll have to turn down the dinner, the movie and the whatever."

"Sorry to hear that."

Was he really, or was it just wishful thinking on her part? "Anyway, thanks for the offer."

"Maybe next time," he offered distractedly before he hung up. Sawyer was evidently not the type to waste words on idle chatter.

She replaced the receiver feeling as though she'd just misplaced a winning lottery ticket. But that was silly. No self-respecting woman would accept a last-minute date with a Western Don Juan like Brody. The guy was clearly on-the-make and the fact that he hadn't set a future date confirmed her earlier suspicions. He simply was not the kind of man she needed in her already complicated life.

When Noelle tucked the boys into bed that night she settled down for another quiet Friday night. She congratulated herself several times for exercising sound judgment in the Brody Sawyer matter and vowed to put him out of her thoughts for good.

She changed into her favorite comfort clothes, an athletic gray lounger that resembled a floor-length sweatshirt, and fuzzy socks. She spared a brief look at the exercise bike mocking her silently from its dusty corner and promptly went into the kitchen to pop some corn. Munchies and a mindless activity such as watching a TV movie were definitely in order.

The movie was half over when the doorbell rang and she had a pretty good idea who was responsible for disturbing her peace. Didn't Steve know better than to try and do his wheedling in person? Since Sunday he'd been *persona non grata* and if he thought he could change her mind about the lawsuit he was mistaken.

She opened the door on the chain, loaded for bear, fully prepared to tell him she'd see him in court.

Chapter Four

Instead Noelle found a grinning Brody leaning against the door jamb. She was so surprised she could only ask the logical question. "What are you doing here?"

"I'm not sure." Brody didn't reveal that he'd been sitting in the truck for half an hour trying to work up the nerve to knock on her door. Since nerve was something he normally had in excess, he had no explanation for that phenomenon, either. Nor did he know why he suddenly turned into a mush-brain when he was near her.

"I've never been turned down for a date before and I guess I'm not handling the rejection very well."

Noelle smiled at his cocky response but made no move to unfasten the chain. He stood on the porch, his hat in his hand, feeling an even bigger fool than he was.

"How did you know where I live?"

"There was only one N. Chandler in the telephone book, so I took a chance." He'd also gambled that she would be glad to see him.

"You weren't just in the neighborhood and decided to drop in?" She couldn't believe the disheveled state he'd caught her in. Her makeup had long since worn off, her hair was caught up in a bumptious ponytail and she had on her ugliest fuzzy socks.

"I felt like some company. I guess it was kinda pushy of me to think you might like some, too. I shouldn't have come."

No, he shouldn't have. But Noelle didn't know why she felt the need to reassure him otherwise. Belatedly, she unlocked the chain and opened the door. "No, no, that's okay."

"Good." He breezed past her and went into the living room of her little house before she could change her mind. Now that he was here he didn't want to be sent packing like some overeager teenager.

He looked around and decided he liked what he saw. The place wasn't a decorator's idea of what a house should look like—it was far too comfortable and lived-in for that—but its warmth made him feel that someone cared more about making a guest feel welcome than about impressing him.

His own house, while spacious and modern, had never seemed very homey. He didn't spend much time there, so maybe that's why the place had a lonesome, empty look to it. Funny, he'd never thought much about such things until he stepped into Noelle's tidy little bungalow, which was exactly the kind of home he expected her to have.

Never one to apologize for his carefully thought-out actions, Brody was a little flapped to hear himself doing so now, after a fashion. "I probably should have called first."

A warning would have been nice. But then, did the Greeks warn the Trojans? Did Sitting Bull warn Custer?

"Have a seat, Brody." Noelle gestured at the easy chair, then sat down stiffly on the sofa.

He opted to sit next to her instead. "Thanks."

She picked up the remote control to switch off the TV set, but he insisted she leave it on. "I don't want to mess up your movie for you. Just go ahead and watch it. Pretend I'm not even here. I can wait until it's over."

Before doing what? she wondered. He smiled at her and focused his attention on the screen as though the only reason he dropped in was to catch the last half of a mediocre movie. She wanted to take his advice, at least until she figured out what he was up to, but there was no way she could ignore him.

Tonight he was dressed in a sharply creased pair of jeans and a white Western shirt that only made his shoulders seem wider. He sat back on the sofa with one ankle crossed over the opposite knee. He was wearing highly polished ostrich boots and his foot was twitching. From time to time he glanced over at her and she found it impossible to reconnect with the story unfolding on the screen.

"You don't mind me keeping you company, do you?" he asked when he caught her watching him.

"No." Why did he ask when he gave every indication of staying? She finally jumped up and, rounding the corner into the kitchen, asked if he'd like a soft drink.

"Got a beer?"

"Root."

"That'll be fine."

When she returned with their drinks she found he'd finished off the popcorn. They continued to watch TV and during the commercials she attempted to fill him in on the parts he'd missed. She only wished someone would fill her in on what she'd missed.

Brody's actions seemed to be motivated by reasons beyond the ken of average people. She distinctly remembered having turned down a date this evening. So exactly how had it happened that he was slouched on her sofa sipping root beer?

Brody hoped Noelle wouldn't notice that he wasn't much interested in the movie and it was hard to pretend that he was. His primary preoccupation was watching Noelle when she thought he wasn't looking. She sure looked cute tonight, as if she were a little girl dressed up in her daddy's shirt.

He'd seen her as a conscientious mother and as a no-nonsense businesswoman, but he liked her best like this. She looked even more vulnerable than usual and he felt a little guilty about wanting so badly to seduce her. But wanting didn't mean he would, and he knew she was safe.

There were lots of reasons why he shouldn't get involved with her, but while he was sitting in Noelle's dimly lit living room, Brody had a hard time recalling what they were.

Oh, yeah. Now he remembered. Dusty and Danny. There were two more hearts to hurt when the relationship ran its course. She was matrimonial—and he definitely wasn't in the market for a wife. He'd seen how much trouble those could be. He'd leave true love to romantics like Riley.

His foster parents, Dub and Ruby, accused him of turning into a crusty old bachelor and at thirty-five they might be right. But better that than to be divorced and dispossessed.

Noelle was about as far from the good sport sort as a woman could get, so a nice friendly affair was probably out of the question. Too bad. The qualities that appealed to him most were the very ones that made her a poor choice for his attentions. That irony was not totally lost on him.

He watched out of the corner of his eye as she shifted against the cushions. It was plain she wasn't wearing a bra and he wondered crazily what, if anything, she did have on under that get-up. He reminded himself that he didn't need to know and tried to concentrate on the movie.

As soon as the closing credits began to roll, Noelle switched off the set. They'd done enough watching; it was time to talk. Maybe Sawyer liked to be mysterious, but she'd have some answers, or he could just go and frustrate somebody else.

"So. Tell me about yourself." If that wasn't short and to the point, she didn't know what was.

"Such as?"

"How'd you happen to become a horse trainer?"

"Just fell into it. My foster parents had horses." Brody knew she didn't mean anything by it, but she said it in the same tone of voice she would have used had she asked, "So tell me, how'd you happen to become an underwater basket weaver?" He tried not to be offended because he knew most people didn't understand the racing business.

"How many horses do you...ah...train?"

"Several." He considered telling her about Cimarron and his success on the circuit, but he wasn't sure how to do it without sounding like he was bragging. He'd learned early that in Dub and Ruby's dictionary, modesty was next to godliness.

"Are you from around here?"

"Oklahoma born and bred."

She sighed. He certainly hadn't displayed such taciturnity when it came to getting personal information out of *her*. She remembered Darcy's question regarding whether or not there were more like him at home. For the sake of the female population she hoped not. "What about family?"

"I have one brother, Riley. Dub and Ruby Roberts took us in when we were just kids, they're our family. Their daughter Glory is like our little sister. But I guess she's not so little anymore. She's away at school now. She plans to be a lady horse vet, not many women in that field. She's one gutsy gal."

"She sounds very determined."

"She is at that. How about you? You got a family?"

"I'm an only child. My parents are divorced. Dad lives in California with his new wife and my mother lives in Tulsa."

"Why don't you live with her? Seems like with the boys and all, you could use the help."

There he went again, asking questions that a civilized person would consider none of his business. "Mother has her own life. She's an executive with an electronics company and doesn't have much time for grandmotherly stuff like baby-sitting. Besides, if I lived any closer I'd have to endure her I-told-you-sos on a daily basis. As it is, twice a month is quite often enough to hear how I married the wrong man and ruined my life."

"Too bad, though, that you don't have anybody to help you."

"I don't need any help."

"So why did you?"

She'd missed something again. "Why did I what?"

"Marry the wrong man. Even if you didn't exactly ruin your life, I take it your ex is a little balky when it comes to support. It's hard for me to understand how a man can be smart enough to marry a woman like you and then be stupid enough to let you get away.''

She grinned wryly. ''There wasn't any 'let' to it. There's a limit to even my tolerance.''

''Have I reached it yet?'' he asked with a grin.

''Just about. But I'll give you the benefit of the doubt if you'll tell me what you're doing here.''

''I couldn't not come.''

He had a disconcerting honesty that Noelle didn't quite know what to make of. ''I see.''

''Tell me more about this ex-husband of yours.''

''Why?''

''So I can understand you.''

No man had ever expressed a desire to understand her before, and she found herself answering Brody's question before she could think of a reason not to. ''Our marriage was a mistake from the beginning, but I blame myself more than Steve for what happened.''

''Go on,'' Brody prompted.

Noelle wasn't sure she wanted to, but his gentle tone encouraged her. ''I should have been the one with better sense. When Steve declared his love for me and asked me to marry him, I actually did him a grave injustice by accepting.''

''Are you always so willing to take on guilt? I thought buck passing was something you learned in middle management.''

She let the jibe go. Noelle understood that most people who didn't work within the establishment, such as Brody, had a healthy disrespect for it. ''Steve wasn't ready for the responsibility, but I thought I could change him. I thought I could give him purpose and I also assumed, incorrectly, that sooner or later we would both want the same things out of life.''

"How so?" He scooted a little closer and studied her intently.

"I wanted a little house with a backyard, stability, kids. The whole suburban cliché was something I didn't have as a child. You know, daddy going off to work and mommy staying home and baking cookies and going to PTA meetings."

"I never had that either," he admitted.

"Well, I thought it was the ideal to strive for and I was willing to work and wait for it. But Steve wanted big money and power. He aspired to the fast lane and it took me a while to realize that wheeler-dealers and dreamers are above honest work."

"There's nothing wrong with having dreams," Brody put in quietly. "I have a few myself. There's a big difference between schemers and dreamers."

She looked at him thoughtfully. "You're right. But Steve's the worst of both. He can't tell the difference between the way he wants things to be and the way things really are. It took me a long time to learn that we just didn't share the same dreams."

Brody was silent for a few moments as though thinking over what she'd just said. "That's a relief."

"What is?"

"That you two parted because of such profound differences. I'd hate to think I was attracted to a woman who'd leave a man because he trimmed his toenails in bed."

After several seconds of consternation, Noelle burst into laughter. Had she worried that things were getting too personal, too serious? Leave it to Brody to make sure that didn't happen.

"So you worked at the bank while your husband spun schemes?" he went on.

"That's about it. He always had a deal cooking, but little ever came of them. Toward the end, I had a full-time job, two babies and bills to pay. I was too busy to care what he was into. Then the oil business bottomed out and the wheeler-dealers slunk back into the woodwork. After that he liked to lie around the house and bemoan his bad luck."

"So how'd you get rid of him?" Brody asked slyly.

"Didn't have to. One day I came home from work and found a convertible in our driveway, the back seat piled high with his stuff. He and his blonde were waiting for me."

"Don't stop there. What did you do?" He winked at her. "I bet you cussed them up one side and down the other."

"I never." She laughed. It was the first time the memory of that day had prompted such a response.

"Fess up, now. Don't forget that I've been on the receiving end of that temper of yours. Did you punch out the blonde?"

"How can you even ask? Civilized people do not punch one another out."

Brody gazed deeply into her eyes and saw a devilish light twinkling there. "You did! You smacked her, didn't you?"

She grinned sheepishly. "Well, she asked for it. I didn't lose control until she started telling me how the boys and I were bad for poor Steve. It was her choice of words that did it. She said she was going to help him realize his dreams."

Brody wished he hadn't brought the subject up. He hated to think she had cared enough for another man to fight for him. "Woman scorned and all that, huh?"

"Not exactly. I'd just had this really bad day at work. Actually, I thanked her for taking the responsibility for Steve's happiness off my shoulders. It was getting to be a full-time job and I already had two of those."

He considered that for such a delicate looking woman, Noelle was one tough customer.

"Let's not talk about him anymore. Tell me more about the Roberts family."

"There isn't much to tell. Dub and Ruby own a quarter horse stallion station near Norman. They gave me and Riley a home when we needed it and they made us part of their family. Ruby tried to teach us manners and morals and Dub taught us everything we know about horses."

From his tone Noelle knew that was all she would hear from him about his personal life—past or present. So she changed the subject and they discussed such things as the changeable weather in Oklahoma and other scintillating topics.

When the conversation lulled, Brody pulled her into his arms. His voice dropped to a throaty level as he said, "Come here, Noelle."

"No, I can't," she whispered. She placed her palms against his chest when all she really wanted to do was melt against him.

He took her hands and put them around his neck. "Hold on. We're gonna do something unusual, but it's something we both need real bad."

"I can't...the boys..." She tried to move away, but he put his hand on the back of her neck and pulled her head down to his broad shoulder.

"It's just a hug," he explained, his lips caressing her temple as he stroked her back.

"Oh," she murmured in a little voice. Instinctively, she tightened her arms around his neck. "A hug? I thought . . ."

"I know what you thought, but you don't have to be afraid of me. I won't force you into anything you don't want."

She sensed his sincerity and felt an overwhelming urge to curl up in his lap. It had been a long time since anyone had been strong for her, since anyone had offered her comfort. It was startling to realize just how much she longed for that. She reached up and stroked his strong jaw and he jerked as if she'd touched him with a hot poker.

Abruptly, he pulled her arms from around his neck and stood. "I'd better get going, while the gettin's good. Well, thanks for the popcorn and the company. And the hug."

When Noelle tried to stand he held up his hand as if he were a traffic cop. "Never mind. I'll let myself out." He strode to the front door, paused, and then came back. He clasped her cheeks in his big work-worn hands and kissed her, quickly but firmly, on the lips. "Good night, Noelle. And thanks again."

Then he was gone, just as unexpectedly as he'd come. Noelle fell back on the sofa, perplexed, and wondered why her little house suddenly seemed so empty. She still felt the pressure of his hug, the security of his arms around her, the heat of the unexpected kiss.

She'd felt the tension building within her all evening and had even worried about how it could be respectably released. She needn't worry about that anymore. She knew exactly how a balloon felt when it made the unexpected acquaintance of a pin.

She had no idea why he'd run out like he had. Was it something she said? Or didn't say? She'd learned a little more about him, but that knowledge only whetted her curiosity. He was a real puzzle. Honest, yet mysterious. Blunt, but sensitive. Kind one minute, curt the next. A woman could go crazy figuring out a man like that. Maybe she shouldn't even try.

Brody waited in his truck until Noelle's lights winked out before he headed home. He didn't know why he was so all fired caught up with her, he only knew that he was.

He felt like a fool for running out when he had. Why had he done such a dumb thing? He'd wined, dined and bedded his share of women, but—not counting Ruby and Glory, of course—she was the first one he'd ever wanted to just hug.

As he drove home he wondered why he was wasting time and energy worrying about the complicated state of his desires. Didn't he have enough trouble, what with Riley falling off the wagon every time he heard a some-body-done-somebody-wrong song?

He should forget about Noelle. Surely he could once he got back to work tomorrow. He had a bunch of young horses in training and the All-American Futurity to pre-pare for. Even if he wanted to, he didn't have the time to court a woman right now.

And if Noelle Chandler wasn't the courting type he'd eat a two-hundred-dollar Stetson.

Chapter Five

Brody drove away from Noelle's house filled with mixed emotions. He prided himself on being a good judge of fillies and knew his assessment had been accurate. She would definitely require a proper courting. Hell, she *deserved* it—and that was the first problem.

Even if he had the inclination for such a prosaic activity, he didn't have the time. At the moment he was busy training the two-year-old he hoped would win the biggest quarter horse race for that class, the All-American Futurity at Ruidoso Downs in New Mexico.

If he could make it happen, he would take home the gleaming silver trophy and the trainer's ten percent of the million-dollar purse for the third year in a row.

This third win was critical. Since horse racing operated on the uncertainty principle, winning big once was usually attributed to luck. Winning twice was still considered by some to be just a happy chance. But winning three times would make the skeptics sit up and take note.

This year could make his reputation and prove once and for all that Brody Sawyer was no flash in the pan.

Now it seemed even his love life operated on the same principle. Meeting Noelle had been an accident of fate. A wrong number—one that he wouldn't even have been in town to answer if not for the problem that had delayed his departure. Normally, this time of year he was already in Ruidoso where his work kept him May through Labor Day with only occasional trips home.

That was another problem. How could he act on the attraction he felt for Noelle when he wouldn't be in the same state? He'd seen the term "commuter relationship" bandied about in the slick magazines he browsed through during flights, but he didn't have the foggiest notion how they worked. He couldn't have met her at a worse time.

Logistics aside, there was an even bigger obstacle in his way. He'd sensed Noelle's disapproval of the work he loved and her unspoken disdain hurt him more than he liked to admit.

Not that she had any idea what it was he really did, or how good he was at it. When it seemed she was jumping to all the wrong conclusions he'd sat there like a knot on a fence post and let her go to it. Why hadn't he told her about Cimarron? About his success? About the trophy cases full of evidence that he was no down-on-his-luck wrangler? He hadn't actually lied about anything, but neither had he told her the whole truth.

Was he afraid that she'd be like the racetrack "groupies," interested in him only when he won? Money and limelight had a strange effect on some women. It was hard to believe that there were females willing to sleep with owners, trainers and jockeys just because they were winners. Rock stars did not have the corner on the bimbo market.

By the time he got home he was willing to admit that maybe his negligence stemmed from fear. That even when Noelle found out he was one of the top trainers on the circuit, she'd still look down her pretty little nose at him. Maybe he was afraid he wouldn't measure up to her lofty expectations or fit her idea of a button-down time-clock puncher.

After lying awake for several hours worrying about the wherefores and why nots, Brody reached a decision. He decided not to decide. Fate had dealt the cards at their meeting, so he would just wait and see if old fate could play the hand. He'd let nature take its course.

The next day he met with the irate horse owner to whom Riley, in one of his more expansive moods, had made some impossible promises. It took a lot of good-ol'-boy finesse, not to mention an expensive lunch at the Steak Joint, to smooth the man's ruffled feathers.

Brody caught a plane that afternoon, hightailing it off to New Mexico where he belonged. He'd be safe there. With so much work to distract him, he could get a certain blonde out of his mind.

For eleven long, gut-wrenching days that's what he told himself. Not that he wasn't vigilant in his attempts to forget Noelle. He reminded himself that she wasn't his type, that she was the marrying kind and had two little boys who seriously needed a full-time resident daddy figure. A role that, while tempting at first glance, was just plain out of the question. One full-time job was enough.

He'd vowed to keep his entanglements, he never called them relationships, light and carefree, but idle vows didn't stand a chance. Not against the memories of how

Noelle had felt in his arms. Not against the *rightness* he'd sensed when he held her. Her soft femininity made him feel strong and virile and elemental. No matter how you looked at it, that was a lot to get from one measley little hug.

As hard as he fought the desire, Brody wanted Noelle Chandler. At least, he told himself, he wanted to explore the possibilities. But it wouldn't be easy, considering her past experience with an entirely different kind of dreamer. He'd have to go slow. She was bound to spook easily, just as easily as the high-spirited horses he trained. He'd win her trust before dumping the truth, the whole truth, and nothing but the truth on her. So help him God.

He came up with a reasonable sounding excuse to return to Oklahoma City and once his plane landed at Will Rogers Airport, he went straight to her front door and knocked. He could be decisive when he decided not to decide something.

It was a few minutes before he heard her muffled voice on the other side.

"Who's there?" she asked, forgetting about the newly installed security viewer.

"Brody."

Noelle peered through the peephole to verify his identity. It was Brody all right. No one wore a cowboy hat with quite the panache he did. This time it was a charcoal gray Stetson that matched his perfectly tailored suede Western-cut sport coat. He had on crisply pressed blue jeans and a white shirt with a bolo tie. She couldn't be sure but the sterling silver clasp looked like a howling coyote.

He grinned into the fish-eye glass with a smile that seemed to say, "Don't be mad, you know you like me." A smile that was so cocky it was almost charming.

Her first impulse was to open the door just for the pleasure of slamming it in his face. Two weeks without a word from him, then here he was sneaking up on her again, catching her off guard and looking better than he had a right to.

"Brody?" she said in a puzzled tone. "Brody who?"

"Sawyer." Hmm. So the lady was ticked that he hadn't called. That was a good sign, wasn't it?

"Oh, yes." Then, so he wouldn't guess just how many flips her stomach had performed when she saw him standing there she added, "The zoo pervert."

"That wasn't exactly how I hoped you'd remember me, but at least you remembered. You gonna let me in?"

She considered the hot curlers in her hair, her shiny, scrubbed face and less than fetching old robe. "I'm thinking about it."

When she saw him shrug and step off the porch, Noelle threw the door open. Suddenly it didn't matter what picture she presented, so long as she could see him again—without a hunk of wood between them.

"I just got back into town," he said without preamble as he stepped into the house. "I thought I'd stop by and see if you wanted to go out for supper."

"Sorry, I'm meeting someone in an hour." She hadn't purposely withheld the information that her "date" was with Darcy but his darkening expression made her glad she had.

"Is this someone you're meeting, special?" Brody asked with studied indifference.

"Oh, yes. Very special." She watched his expression go positively black before adding, "Darcy Durant is my best friend. She'd be very disappointed if I didn't show up."

She? He was so relieved that Noelle wasn't meeting some guy that he forgave her misleading remarks. "I guess this is short notice."

"Again," she reminded.

"I probably should have called." He stood with his hat in his hand, wondering why he didn't just hit the road. The lady's dance card was all filled up for the evening.

"Definitely."

"That's how things are done, huh?" he asked so ingenuously that Noelle smiled in spite of her earlier chagrin.

"Among civilized people. Sit down, Brody. I have to ask you a serious question."

He took a seat cautiously, filled with a sudden anxiety as to what that question might be. "Yeah?"

She took his hands in hers and looked deeply into his eyes. Today green dominated over brown in the hazel irises. "Do you have some deep-seated phobia regarding Mr. Bell's invention? Because if you do, I think we'd better deal with it right now."

He laughed and his relief that she wasn't really mad at him showed. "It was an impulse. Telephones get in the way of impulses."

Noelle had to forgive him—up close and personal was much better than hearing a voice over a wire. "It's been almost two weeks since I last heard from you. I assumed you weren't interested in seeing me again."

"I'm interested. Too interested." The pleasure he was feeling at seeing her now was so intense, even with those bumpy things in her hair, that Brody couldn't understand why he'd waited.

"I'm afraid you'll have to explain that one."

"I spend more time out of town than I do in it. I'm in New Mexico all summer and the rest of the time I'm on the southwestern circuit for one race or another. My life-style doesn't exactly inspire lasting relationships and I got the impression that those were the only kind you were interested in.''

"Just a tumbling tumbleweed, huh? If that's the message you got, why did you come here tonight?''

"I came because I had to see you again. I want to get to know you." He looked at her levelly and his gaze melted into hers. "In every way.''

The implication of his words caught her off guard. "You like to get right to the heart of the matter, don't you?''

"I'm an up-front kind of guy, I don't have time for games. So, how about it? Would you like to get to know me better?''

"Considering what you just told me, won't that be a little difficult?" His nearness seemed to steal her breath and her pulses beat so rapidly she felt as if she'd been walking uphill—fast.

"Maybe, but I think it would be worth the effort. For both of us.''

"I have the boys to consider.''

"I know. I've thought about them, too. If we go into this with our eyes open, with no promises and no strings, no one has to get hurt.''

She wanted to believe that. "No deposit, no return?" She'd only had one serious involvement in her life and it had resulted in marriage. She didn't know if she could deal with the concept of disposable relationships.

"Exactly," he concurred. "Forget the long-term and think about the here and now. What would it hurt for us to have some fun together?" He looked at her closely. "You can have fun, can't you?''

"I've been known to—when coerced.''

"Great. Coercion is my middle name. So how about tonight?"

"I promised Darcy I'd attend her performance tonight. She's a singer."

He nodded and shrugged, unable to completely hide his disappointment. "How about tomorrow? I won't be in the city long."

"I hate leaving the boys with a sitter two nights in a row." Despite the little pep talk he'd just given her about living for today, Noelle was afraid she'd regret her next question tomorrow. "Would you like to go with me?"

His grin spread slowly. "I'd like." Suddenly remembering that he hadn't eaten since breakfast, Brody asked. "Can I grab something to eat there?"

"You could, but the boys and I were just about to sit down to dinner. How do you feel about pizza?"

"Sounds great. It's one of my favorite food groups."

They were interrupted when the boys skidded into the room. "Yea!" Dusty shouted. "It *is* him."

"Awright!" Danny looked up at Brody. "I told Dusty it was you."

"I said it first," Danny replied.

"Did not."

"Did so."

Noelle gave Brody a long suffering smile. "Are you two going to stay in here and argue or will you calm down and have some pizza with us?"

"Are you really gonna eat here?" Dusty wanted to know with a wide-eyed wonder that said he thought communal dining was the first step toward daddyhood.

Brody tossed his hat on the sofa and bent down on one knee. "If it's okay with you guys."

"It's okay with us." Dusty turned Brody's cheek in his direction with his little hand. "Are you gonna take Momma to hear our Darcy sing?"

"Yep," Brody drawled in his best cowboy voice.

"Yippee!"

In their unabashed excitement the boys squeezed his neck and something tightened in Brody's heart. He hadn't dreamed that soap-scented hugs could have such an effect him. When he glanced at Noelle she was frowning. "At least someone's pleased about it," he quipped.

She found his instant rapport with her sons a bit disconcerting. If things didn't work out, she could live with the disappointment. She was free to make mistakes, if that's what Brody was, but Dusty and Danny were another matter. They'd been hurt before and it was up to her to see that it didn't happen again.

She chided herself for making more of Brody's presence than she should. She was as bad as Danny when it came to making quantum leaps in logic. Trying to sound cheerful, Noelle said, "I hear a pizza calling us."

"Ah, Momma," Dusty lamented. "Pizzas can't talk."

But little boys certainly could. Their lively chatter prevented the adults from having any serious thoughts or conversation with their dinner. Brody had hoped to drop a few hints about what he'd been doing for the past two weeks, but he didn't get a chance.

"We peeked out of our bedroom when you were here last time," Danny informed Brody, trying to invoke as much solemnity as his pizza-smeared face would permit. "And when we saw you huggin' on Momma, Dusty thought you was gonna be our new dad."

"So did Danny," his brother put in. "But Momma 'splained that you'd prob'ly never be anybody's dad."

"I explained," Noelle quickly interjected, "that with your busy life-style, parenthood most likely wasn't in your plans." Embarrassed, she turned to the boys and said, "If you've finished eating, wash up and brush your teeth."

"After that can we show Brody our room?" Dusty asked.

"Please?" Danny chimed.

Noelle cleared the table and loaded the dishwasher, activities designed to keep her busy and out from under Brody's scrutiny. "I don't think he's interested," she said softly.

Says who? "I'm dying to see your room, guys," Brody told the twins seriously. The boys were valuable allies and he sensed he'd need all the help he could get. His only experience with children had been with Riley's stepchildren, but he knew better than to use those little darlings as yardsticks by which to measure normal kids.

He followed the twins into the bathroom to oversee their well-intentioned scrubbing and marveled at the wonder of the tiny hands held up for his inspection. When they finished brushing their teeth, they opened their mouths wide for his approval of a job well-done.

"Good work, boys," he commended, feeling momentarily overwhelmed by the innocent sweetness of what was obviously a nightly ritual. His throat tightened when he couldn't recall a similar one from his own childhood. Had anyone ever cared enough about him to worry about cavities?

"You can kiss us if you wanna," Dusty offered with a wide grin. "Momma always does. She likes fresh toothpaste kisses."

"Yeah," Danny enthused. "They're the best kind."

"I'll have to remember that." Brody pecked each boy in turn and decided there was something sweet about the act, but he didn't think it could be attributed strictly to the toothpaste.

A few minutes later he found himself in their bedroom trying to figure out how to respond to all their "lookits" and "watch me's."

"You wanna color?" Danny pulled a cigar box from a shelf and plopped it on a child-size table in the corner. "We gots some neat Batman coloring books."

Dusty pulled out a tiny chair. "You can sit in my chair, Brody."

"Sit in mine, it's bigger." Danny pulled out a chair exactly like his brother's.

"Ain't neither."

"Is so."

Brody cut in, "I'm afraid I'm too big for your chairs, guys."

The boys appeared to consider that. "Yeah," said Dusty. "You might break it down like Goldilocks did the baby bear's chair."

"That's right. Why don't you sit in the chairs and I'll sit on the floor."

"Yeah," they chorused. "We'll all sit on the floor." With that Dusty and Danny plopped down beside Brody and began explaining the intricacies of staying inside the lines.

When Noelle finished the dishes she went straight to her room to dress. She glanced in the mirror and laughed at the unadorned face she saw there. What had Brody been thinking when he said he wanted to get to know her better? She was surprised he hadn't taken one look at her and ridden right back out of town again.

She sat down at the dressing table and swore that when she was finished she'd knock his socks off. She'd make him glad he'd hung around.

The club where Darcy was performing tonight was a cut above the usual joints, so Noelle dressed in her newest outfit—a fringed sand-colored suede skirt and vest, worn with a dark turquoise silk shirt and knee-high suede boots.

It was a far cry from her standard wardrobe choices, but when she'd seen it at the little shop in the mall, she'd thought of Brody. At the time, Noelle didn't think she'd ever hear from him again, but she'd succumbed to an unfamiliar impulse and bought it anyway.

Now, as she twirled in front of the full-length mirror, she was glad she'd gotten so carried away. The ensemble made her look much more confident than she felt.

When the sitter arrived Noelle wrote down the phone number where she could be reached and left Mrs. Sterling watching television while she went to fetch the boys. She opened the door and was surprised to find Brody's dark head sandwiched between two small blond ones as they bent over coloring books.

"Mrs. Sterling is here, boys," she announced after drinking in her fill of the sight. "Come and say hello."

Dusty and Danny dropped their crayons and bounded out of the room, scattering half-colored portraits of Batman under their bare feet.

Brody stood, transfixed by the lovely woman standing in the doorway. This was no banker lady he was dealing with tonight. With her blond hair shining and turquoise-and-silver earrings flashing, he thought she was by far the prettiest woman he'd ever seen.

"You clean up pretty good," he said in hopes of dispelling the tension between them.

She laughed self-consciously. "Was that a compliment? With you, it's hard to tell sometimes."

"It sure was. You look great."

"Thanks. But I don't look too much like Annie Oakley, do I?" she asked, suddenly unsure about the fringe and the concho belt. "Do I look like I might break out with a few bars of 'You Can't Get a Man With a Gun'?"

"Nope. Any woman who looks as good as you do, doesn't need a gun."

Noelle knew she was blushing again. "What were you doing down there?"

He stacked the books and put the scattered crayons back in the box. "We were coloring."

"You didn't have to do that."

"The boys wanted me to and I didn't mind."

"I'll bet it's been a few years since you've done it."

"Actually, I was just thinking that I never had."

"You're kidding."

"I guess Riley and I were too busy surviving to waste time on such things." He said it offhandedly, as if trying to reduce the impact of the words. Maybe she was reading too much into them, but Noelle sensed regret and longing and a little bitterness, as well.

She'd been pampered and spoiled by her divorced parents, who had sought to make up for their self-absorption by keeping her so busy with activities and material goods that she wouldn't notice their inattention. Survival had never been an issue in her life and she had difficulty visualizing the kind of childhood Brody and Riley must have had.

She wanted to question him further, but she knew better than to pry. She could only hope he'd eventually feel comfortable enough to share some of his life with her.

As Brody drove to the club Noelle silently marveled at the plush interior of his dusty pickup truck. It was equipped with lush upholstery on reclining seats, automatic windows, door locks and a state-of-the-art sound system.

All she'd heard about cowboys prizing their trucks was true. It was possible that this vehicle represented most of Brody's net worth.

She felt his gaze on her and her pulses kicked into high gear again. When she glanced up he turned his attention back to his driving. He asked her questions about her work and they chatted amiably until they reached the club.

Cowboy's Restaurant and Club was a favorite of local country-western music fans. Besides great food, it boasted an excellent sound system and oversize dance floor, which was designed to accommodate all the two-steppers who cared to show off their style.

It was a step up for Darcy and her small band to perform in a place where the ambience included snowy linen tablecloths and soft lighting. They usually worked clubs in which clattering beer bottles and clouds of cigarette smoke disguised acoustic and decorating shortcomings.

Once they were seated at a table near the dance floor, Noelle turned to Brody. "Darcy is very talented and I'm glad she got booked here."

"Does she have plans to record?" he asked.

"She's hopeful. She's planning to spend her vacation on Music Row in Nashville. She's leaving next week to check out the possibilities."

"Maybe she'll get lucky."

"I hope so. She deserves it."

He scooted his chair closer to Noelle's and they talked about the safe subject of Darcy's career ambitions until a waitress appeared and introduced herself as Pam. They declined to see a menu, but Brody ordered a bottle of wine.

The girl turned around, still writing on her pad, and ran smack into a tall, handsome young man who'd stepped up behind her. "Well, if it isn't no-show Riley," she said with good-natured censure.

"What's the matter, honey, did we have a date or something?" he asked in a deep voice that was surprisingly like Brody's.

"Something like that," she muttered as she flounced past him. "Excuse me, unlike some people, I have work to do."

Riley watched her for a moment, then shrugged. "Pam, honey," he called. "Bring me a beer when you come back." He turned his smile full force on Brody and Noelle who'd overheard the exchange. "Hi, big brother. You lookin' for me?"

"Not tonight." Brody offered Riley a chair and introduced Noelle. "Are you alone?"

"For the time being." Riley grinned. From the way his brown eyes twinkled and charmed, Noelle knew that would be a temporary state. "Small world, huh?"

"*We* came to hear the singer," Brody said, his tone indicating that Riley's intentions were somehow less honorable.

Noelle sensed the tension and put in, "Darcy's my best friend. This is her first time here."

"I hear she's good," Riley said absently, keeping his intent gaze on Noelle. "I've never seen you here before, have I?"

Brody's arm went around her shoulder possessively. "Cut it out, Riley. She's *my* date."

"I know that." His semi-apology was marred by a devilish wink.

Noelle smiled her acceptance. Riley was more than a little ornery but not unlike his older brother. She couldn't understand why Brody kept frowning at him. Especially when he downed his beer and ordered another. She'd mistakenly thought Brody was the beer type also, but he seemed content to sip chablis as the threesome chatted companionably.

Before long Darcy was introduced and she stepped up to the microphone amid enthusiastic applause. She wore boots, a pair of snug jeans and a rhinestone-studded denim vest over a full-sleeved pink shirt. Her long black hair, styled in a riot of curls, swung and bounced as she romanced the audience.

Noelle glanced at Riley and it was easy to see that he was entranced by her friend.

Darcy's first number was "Desperado," a song about a man who refused to let anyone love him. A man so blinded by the pursuit of freedom he couldn't see that his prison was walking through the world all alone.

Noelle stole a glance at Brody and wondered if he realized how much he was like the man immortalized in the song. She didn't know him as well as she wanted to, but she sensed his troubled heart.

He seemed open and outgoing, but in the short time she'd spent with him she'd come to see the jokes and laughter as a refuge where he hid from those who might want to get too close to him. There was definitely more to Brody Sawyer than met the eye and she didn't know if she was up to plumbing the depths.

When her set was finished, Darcy joined the threesome. Riley's interest was reciprocated by the fast-talking brunette and from the moment they were introduced, they literally had neither eyes nor ears for anyone else.

Brody leaned close to Noelle. "Do you want to dance?" he called over the loud music as the band struck up a cotton-eyed joe.

"Do you think we'll be missed?" she asked facetiously.

Brody looked at the couple who had scooted their chairs together for private communication. "They've forgotten all about us."

With a hand on her lower back, he guided Noelle onto the floor. Her awareness of him intensified with every step they took and by the time he led her into the dance, she was aching with suppressed feelings. She wasn't as comfortable with the set steps as he was, but his gentle instructions and sense of humor soon overcame her self-consciousness.

When the music stopped they stayed on the floor and waited for the next number, a two-step. Brody was a good dancer and his big sinuous body led her through the steps with ease. When he wrapped her in his arms for a slow dance, his nearness unleashed the pent-up emotions she had sought to control.

Chest to chest, thigh to thigh, they swayed dreamily to the heart-wrenching sad song as lights twinkled overhead like stars brought indoors. One of his work-roughened hands branded the small of Noelle's back while the other carried her hand up to his neck. With both arms around her, he tightened his hold and drew her close, bringing their bodies into delicious contact.

Noelle was more than a little threatened by the intensity of her response to Brody but being held in his arms was a treat she wasn't prepared to deny herself. It had been so long since she'd felt close to a man and she re-veled in this one's strength and warmth.

She giggled at the silly things he whispered in her ear and felt like a young girl again. She was just twenty-nine, but she'd been responsible and tough for so long that she'd almost forgotten how to have fun—how to enjoy a man's company—how to feel utterly like a woman.

With Brody she felt desired and entrancing. She was a hardworking single mother of two who was often so tired at the end of the day that she fell into bed exhausted. But Brody made her feel special and gave her back some of the confidence that Steve had stolen from her.

It was probably wrong to give that much power to a man she scarcely knew. He'd said no strings, no promises, and Noelle knew better than to invest her emotions in him. But right or wrong, there was no place she'd rather be at this moment than in his arms.

Chapter Six

One slow dance melted into another. Noelle soon lost herself in the music and the potent magnetism of Brody's body. Lifting her head from his chest, she peered up into his face. The tenderness she saw there made her forget, temporarily, all her reservations about him. No man had ever looked at her with the kind of yearning she saw in his eyes. The effect was exciting and dazzling.

Words became extraneous as they clung together, paying more attention to the nuances of their movements than to the changing tempo of music that seemed to fade into background noise. Every cliché Noelle had ever heard about time standing still was brought to bear on the minutes that slipped away, unnoticed and unheeded.

When Brody dipped his head and kissed her lightly, she didn't even think of pulling away; relaxing in his embrace was the only logical response. He caressed her lips with his thumb, whether to rescind the kiss or seal it there forever, she couldn't tell. She waited, her heart hammering in anticipation of another, more thorough, kiss.

"Don't look now, cowboy," Darcy murmured as she and Riley passed on their way back to the table. "But the band done took a break."

Brody and Noelle jumped apart guiltily and he guided her back to their chairs without a word. Darcy was waiting, purse in hand.

"Come to the ladies' room with me," she told Noelle in a tone indicating the necessity of the "girls only" jaunt. They were scarcely out of earshot when Darcy quipped, "Brody must be a *real* cowboy."

"I don't think that's ever been in question," Noelle responded dryly.

Once in the brightly lit ladies' room, Darcy applied fresh lip gloss. "Only real cowboys dance with their hats on. I wonder what else he does with his hat on?"

"If you're thinking what I think you're thinking, I won't be finding out." When Noelle looked into the mirror and saw her flushed face, she recalled just how carried away she'd been out on the dance floor. Brody had worked a spell over her, but thank goodness for bright lights. They were a great restorer of reality.

"Why not?" Darcy persisted. "You're both grownups."

"Brody's all wrong for me."

"Says who?"

"He's not looking for a commitment. He told me so."

Darcy looked at her friend closely. "And is a commitment so important to you?"

"I have to think of the boys. They need a father—one that'll stay in one place."

"So instead of thinking about what a man can give you, you're looking for a father for Danny and Dusty. Is that the criteria by which you judge every man you meet?''

"It's one consideration," Noelle said defensively.

"Look, honey, I don't have any kids, so it's easy for me to preach. But you have to satisfy yourself first. And if what I saw out there on that dance floor is any indication, Brody Sawyer is satisfaction on the hoof."

"You certainly seemed to hit it off with Riley." Noelle deftly changed the subject. She didn't like thinking about what Darcy said. And she didn't like admitting it was true.

Darcy frowned. "The chemistry between us is the stuff of legends, but that's one romance story that'll never be written."

"Why not? He seems like a nice kid."

"That 'kid' is thirty-one years old and bad news."

"Really?" Noelle was genuinely surprised. Not that she doubted Darcy already knew all of Riley's vital statistics, she was an expert at getting people to talk about themselves. No, what was surprising was that Riley was only four years younger than Brody. Though he was often brash and sometimes downright silly, Brody had a maturity that seemed lacking in his brother.

"Yeah, really. I could handle him being a flirt and a rounder, which he definitely is. When you've worked as many joints as I've worked, you learn to pick 'em out in a crowd."

"So what's the problem? He seems attracted to you."

Darcy sighed, a bit regretfully. "Now there's an understatement for you. But he scares the bejeesus out of me."

"I never figured you for a coward where men are concerned." Not like me, Noelle added silently. Despite their differences, or perhaps because of them, she and Darcy had been close friends for nearly five years. It was a commonly espoused belief, at least among hairdressers, that blondes had more fun. Boy, did they have a lot to learn.

Sexy, wise-cracking Darcy had all the fun she could handle. She often accused Noelle of being too conservative and conventional. She was always exhorting her to lighten up. So if Darcy, the original live-and-let-live kid, thought Riley was bad news, he probably was.

Darcy tossed her hair. "That's the problem. In a lot of ways he's not a man yet. He's still a boy that someone needs to take to raise and I don't have the time." Her serious demeanor suddenly vanished. "Suitability quotients, be damned. The brothers Sawyer are two cute hombres. Let's get back out there before some other heifers brand 'em."

Noelle laughed at her friend's colorful, if mixed, metaphor. "I thought you said you didn't want to take him to raise?"

"I don't. But a girl's entitled to a little fun. He'll make a nice playmate. For one evening, anyway."

They returned to the table and the four of them indulged in light-hearted conversation until Darcy took the stage for her next set. Both Noelle and Brody noted how taken Riley was with the violet-eyed singer. He couldn't take his eyes off her. When she sang a song about a man who had the touch that lit a fire way down deep in her soul, she seemed to sing it just for him.

Brody and Noelle refrained from talking during the set, and she realized just how little they had talked. She had met him nearly three weeks ago and still knew next to nothing about his work. Which was funny, considering how the first thing most people shared, after introductions, was their jobs. In the business world, what a person did sometimes seemed more important than who that person was.

Brody wasn't part of that world, so she shouldn't judge him by those standards. It was refreshing not to have her professional life intrude on her personal life for a change.

Of course, she speculated, he might be hiding some big dark secret. Like the fact that on his income tax form he listed CIA hit man under occupation. She stole a quick glance at him and immediately discarded that ridiculous theory. Brody was too big-hearted to hurt anyone and too forthright to ever do anything dishonest.

More likely, he didn't like to talk about his work because he wasn't proud of being a thirty-five-year-old horse groomer. He'd mentioned having dreams, so he wasn't totally lacking in ambition. Noelle chided herself for such an uncharitable thought. She wasn't a profession snob, so why was she thinking like one?

Still, she had to wonder. Riley had made a comment about heading back to "the spread" later and when she'd asked if they worked together, Brody's brother had looked at her funny and said, "Well, sure." Brody had whisked her off to the dance floor and made her forget all about asking questions. *Was* he hiding something?

So what? She had a few secrets of her own, although admittedly not as many as she'd had before he'd sweet-talked her out of her life story.

She felt his gaze and when she looked up, he smiled happily. As soon as Darcy left the stage to deafening applause, he grabbed Noelle's hand and led her across the dance floor.

"We can't dance," she protested. "The band's on break."

"There's a jukebox over there and I'm going to feed it some quarters so it'll play something slow and easy.

That'll give me a good excuse to hold you." He stroked her cheek. "Do you have a problem with that?"

She shook her head. That was one of the few things she *didn't* have a problem with. She wrapped her arms around his neck and nestled her cheek against his chest in a gesture that was quickly becoming familiar. She settled against him and felt the erratic cadence of his heart under her cheek. This was obviously what the inventors of dancing had in mind when they'd first come up with the idea.

The intimacy ended when the band came back and struck up a fast tune. Brody grinned down at her and clasping his arm around her shoulders guided her back to their table. Instead of sitting down he took some bills from his pocket and laid them on the table. They said goodbye to Darcy and Riley and stepped out into the warm, starry night.

When they arrived at Noelle's the boys were in bed and sound asleep. Mrs. Sterling was draped over the living room sofa, her glasses all askew. One of her no-nonsense shoes was upside down beneath the coffee table and the other was still on the foot that never made it to the couch. With each indrawn breath she let loose a loud snore.

"Looks like the boys flat wore her down to nothing," Brody whispered.

"Maybe it was the other way around. If Dusty and Danny weren't exhausted, they'd never be able to sleep through all that snoring," she said with an indulgent smile.

"It's a shame to wake her."

"I know. But I usually call Mr. Sterling and he comes for her."

"I could take her home," he offered, anxious to be alone with Noelle. He hadn't begrudged Riley's or

Darcy's company tonight, but he sure wanted a few quiet moments without distractions. But what happened once he left to take Mrs. Sterling home? He couldn't very well come back. Not without an invitation, anyway.

"That's kind of you, thanks."

"You're welcome," he said halfheartedly. Now he'd even missed his chance for a good-night kiss because Noelle immediately leaned over and gently shook the old lady's shoulders. That's what he got for being a Good Samaritan.

"What? Who did that?" Mrs. Sterling sat up with a jerk, fumbling to adjust her glasses. When she saw Noelle she explained hastily, "I wasn't asleep, dear. I was just resting my eyes."

"That's okay, Mrs. Sterling." Noelle helped the woman slip on her other shoe.

"Is Burt here already?" She blinked and glanced around, barely aware of her surroundings.

"No, I didn't call him. Mr. Sawyer offered to see you home."

"Well, I don't know." Mrs. Sterling patted her hair and fidgeted with her skirt. "I only met him for the first time tonight."

"Not to worry, dear." Noelle patted her hands. "I'll vouch for his trustworthiness."

"Mercy me, I didn't mean to imply..." Mrs. Sterling fretted. "I'm sure he's...I mean whatever will Burt think?"

"Mr. Sterling will be glad he doesn't have to come out so late," Noelle said gently. "But if it would make you feel better, I'll call him and say you're on your way home. That way he can turn on the porch light and watch for you."

Brody smiled at the woman to assure her that he hid no Jack the Ripper tendencies and offered her a hand up. She hesitated only briefly before allowing him to tug her to her feet. She turned to make sure that Noelle was indeed calling her husband as they started toward the door.

Brody rolled his eyes heavenward when Noelle flashed him a smile of gratitude. "Oh, by the way, where does she live?" he asked.

"Next door." Her grin turned ornery as she spoke into the phone.

The look he gave her as he escorted Mrs. Sterling out the door told her to expect him back. When he came she'd simply send him on his way. It was the only safe thing to do. All that so-called dancing had stirred up feelings she'd rather leave alone.

Brody was not the kind of man who would welcome those feelings. He'd made it clear that he wanted a no-strings relationship, but she wasn't sure she could handle such casualness. Brody wasn't looking for love.

But in all honesty, Noelle *was*. She didn't have to have a man to feel happy and fulfilled, but if she was going to have to deal with one on a regular basis he'd darn sure better love her. She wanted someone to share life with, to make a home for, to be there for her and the boys. Brody, as charming as he was, just wasn't a likely candidate.

If she saw much more of him, she'd do something dumb like fall in love with him and that would be the end of a wonderful friendship. No, better to nip it in the bud, to send him away before someone got hurt. It wasn't as if she didn't know who that someone was likely to be.

When Brody knocked lightly a few moments later, Noelle knew what she had to do. Vowing to be strong, she squared her shoulders and opened the door.

But something happened when she saw him draped lazily against the doorframe and she forgot all about sending him away. Maybe they should talk first. "Come in," she invited softly.

"I wasn't sure I'd be welcome."

"I didn't get a chance to tell you how much I enjoyed the evening. I really had a good time."

"And I didn't get a chance to say goodbye." He took a step toward her, but she was afraid of what that goodbye might entail and quickly invited him to sit down.

He patted the cushion beside him. "Join me."

It was stronger than an invitation, softer than a demand, and she knew that if she accepted she'd lose her resolve. "What I have to say will be easier if I'm standing."

Brody, who'd been leaning back against the plump cushions, sat up straight. "Uh-oh. This sounds serious."

"It is." Her hands, the shaky traitors, kept getting in the way so she folded them behind her back. "I don't think we should see each other again."

"I thought you said you had a good time."

"I did. But I think it would be better for both of us if we just ended things now."

"When we discussed this earlier, you seemed agreeable enough. No deposit, no return?" he prompted. "What changed your mind?" He wasn't about to give up easily. The time he'd spent with her, which could still be measured in hours, was too important to just let go. He needed more time.

"You overwhelm me," she admitted honestly. "I'm not sure I can keep my end of the bargain." It cost her but she said it.

"Sit down, Noelle. I promise not to grab." She complied and Brody tried to decipher her body language, which had to make more sense than her verbal cues. "What are you afraid of?"

What was she afraid of? She was afraid to fall in love with this man and she was afraid he would break her inexperienced heart. If Brody ran true to type, all she had to do was tell him exactly what was on her mind. But she wasn't ready for that much vulnerability, so she hedged her bets.

"I'm afraid to fall in love with you. I think it would be a big mistake."

Brody smiled as a surge of relief flooded through him. A woman had actually mentioned love and him in the same sentence and he wasn't heading for the door. Maybe this could work out after all.

"Is that all?" Smiling, he tipped her chin up. "Don't worry about that. I'm not that easy to fall in love with. I'm ornery. I eat Fig Newtons in bed. I never hang up my clothes and I've been known to leave wet towels on the floor until mildew grew on them.

"I'm hardheaded, opinionated and stubborn as a rock post. I actually like pickled pigs' feet. I have zilch interest in intellectual matters and no taste whatsoever for the finer things in life."

He paused in his anti-Brody tirade and Noelle laughed in spite of her overwrought emotions. "What are you trying to tell me, Brody?"

He cupped her face in his hands. "I'm trying to tell that a smart, good-looking banker lady like you doesn't have to worry about falling in love with a horsey good ol' boy like me. You're too good for me."

He certainly knew how to defuse a potentially explosive moment. She made a face at him. "Brody?"

"Yeah?"

"I think you missed the point."

Did that mean she was already falling for him? He could only hope. After all, he'd made a damn good argument against himself. "Answer me true, Noelle Chandler, did you or did you not have fun tonight?"

"Yes, but—"

"Enough said."

"But—"

"Are you feeling a little confused?"

She nodded slowly and he eased her back into his arms. Smiling tenderly he leaned forward and brought her face toward his, whispering against her lips, "Let's see if we can clarify something."

Maybe if he hadn't been so humble and appealing, maybe if he'd kissed her forcefully, she'd have had a chance. But there was nothing at all threatening about the way his warm breath fanned her hair. There was nothing to censure about the gentle kisses he applied to her eyelids, the tip of her nose, her chin. There was only a promise of more to come.

By the time he arranged her more comfortably in his arms and his mouth finally found her trembling lips, she was limp with desire. She had also forgotten why she'd wanted to send him away.

His fingers caressed her temples, then nestled in her hair as he drew her closer to him. Noelle lost herself in the embrace and surrendered to the magic of his kisses.

Brody had tried to lighten the tension between them, but there was no way he could joke about the effect Noelle had on him. Put simply, he was on fire for her. He held her close as he slowly unbuttoned the top buttons of her blouse, then sighed his need as he buried his face in the silken warmth of her neck.

"I have to be honest with you, Noelle," he murmured. "I want you more than I've ever wanted anyone. If that scares you, I'm sorry."

"Brody..."

"Do you want me?" he insisted.

No, no, her few remaining shreds of logic insisted. But how could she lie at a moment like this? Brody made her feel like a beautiful, desirable woman and it had been a long time since she'd been stirred so deeply. Her ragged response, when she was finally able to make it, was not a denial. "Yes, yes."

With urgency born of desire he deepened the kiss and slid his hand between their bodies to cup her breast in his palm. Noelle thrilled to the intimacy of his touch and her breast grew firm and full, even as the rest of her melted with pleasure. She felt as if her body had been designed exclusively for his touch.

Emotion blazed through Brody like an Oklahoma grass fire, but he fought to contain his ardor. Gently, slowly, he pushed aside the silky fabric of her blouse until her breast surged tautly, until her arousal blossomed beneath his fingertips.

Her lips were now a sweet flame that threatened to burn out of control. Brody tore his mouth from hers, kissing her cheek, her neck, her shoulders.

She reveled in his mastery. His lips, his tongue, his touch, became a part of her—an essential part of her. She breathed in his manly scent and savored his masculinity.

Perhaps she already did love him. The taste of his lips still lingered on hers, but when she felt his warm breath on her breast, it took all the willpower she could muster to pull away from him.

"Please, Brody. Don't." Her words were little more than a token protest, but they were enough to drag him from the depths of passion.

"Noelle." He whispered her name on a sigh as he lowered his head to her chest in resignation.

"I can't," she tried to explain as she rebuttoned her shirt.

"Wait, don't move yet," he said as his arms went around her. "Just let me hold you for a minute."

The way she felt right now, he could hold her forever if he wanted. But he only asked for a minute. She was grateful he'd respected her wishes, but she already felt bereft.

When his breathing finally slowed Brody raised his head. It was too soon. He'd rushed her. Exactly what he'd sworn not to do. She needed more time, hell he needed more time. Maybe the moment was right to set her straight about a few things—mainly, his goals, dreams and financial status.

"Noelle, there's something I need to tell you. It's important."

She gazed up at him, still flushed from the warmth of his kisses. "Not now, Brody." She didn't want to spoil the moment with rationalizations or explanations, so she kissed the words away.

The plea in her voice, as much as the unexpected kiss, made Brody honor her request, even though doing so caused a fresh wave of guilt to wash over him. He felt like a heel for not telling her about Cimarron before this.

There was no excuse for withholding such information, and the longer he postponed it the harder it would be to come clean. His was a sin of omission, but it was dishonest just the same.

She saw the look on his face and interpreted it incorrectly. She should have called a halt to his advances sooner. She didn't want Brody to think she ran hot and cold. "I'm sorry," she mumbled.

"I'm sorry, too," he replied in an unintentionally gruff voice.

She watched him get to his feet and pick up his hat. Seemed he couldn't wait to get away from her. Obviously, his idea of "having a little fun" wasn't the same as hers. "I think we're sorry for entirely different reasons," she whispered as the door shut behind him.

Chapter Seven

Darcy was excited when she returned from Nashville. She told Noelle about the contacts she had made there and confided that if not for her family, she'd be tempted to leave the security of her bank job to try her luck in the music business.

A week later her mother, who suffered from severe and chronic arthritis, stumbled on the stairs and broke her leg. After that, Darcy quit talking about Nashville.

Noelle knew how hard it was for her friend to relinquish her dreams but admired her devotion to family. The tragedy of Darcy's late father's alcoholism had made Darcy strong and unselfish. It had also made the survivors, Darcy, her mother and younger brother, closer than any family Noelle knew.

One day over lunch in the bank's break room, Noelle asked her casually if she'd seen Riley since she'd been back.

"A few times."

"Do you like him."

"I guess so."

Normally loquacious, Darcy's terse answers were a sign of trouble and Noelle knew it. "What's wrong?"

"Everything," she admitted. "Riley can be sweet and charming and sexy as hell."

"It must run in the family," Noelle said wryly.

"It sounds stupid, but my heart pounds when I'm with him. I jump every time I hear the phone ring because it might be him. I can't concentrate on anything for thinking about him."

Noelle smiled. "I know the feeling. So, what's the problem?"

Darcy set down her cup of tea. Besides decaffeinated coffee, it was the strongest thing Noelle had ever seen her drink. "You really don't know, do you?"

"Know what?"

"Riley's a drunk, Noelle."

Darcy's words startled her. "Are you sure?"

She sighed. "I'm a veteran, remember? I lived with my father for twenty years and the last fifteen of those were sheer hell. I think I know a drunk when I see one."

"Brody said he was having some problems getting over his divorce, but he never let on that things were so bad."

"Of course not. The alcoholic and his family always deny it at first. It's just a little drinking problem. It's only temporary. It'll go away. I've heard it all before."

"There must be something Brody can do," Noelle said in a worried voice.

"Oh, no. The only one who can help Riley is Riley. He has to admit he needs help, and then he has to get it—himself. But he won't do either one of those things because he's too damn stubborn."

"That's what you meant about not taking him to raise, wasn't it?" When Darcy nodded, she continued, "I'm amazed that you recognized the problem at your first meeting. I didn't sense anything amiss."

"As I recall, you were a little preoccupied with another Sawyer brother that night," Darcy said with a gentle smile. "Riley really admires Brody. He says if it hadn't been for him, he might not have made it. He feels he's let Brody down somehow, that he can't measure up. I don't know what all happened to them when they were kids, but whatever it was, it was bad."

Noelle recalled the few times Brody had mentioned his childhood and agreed. "Brody worries about Riley, I do know that much."

"Yeah, well, Riley needs somebody to worry about him. He's trying every way he knows how to destroy himself. I won't let him take me down with him. I've got Mom and Cord to think of. I can't let myself get too involved. Even if I do love him," she added softly.

"You're in love with Riley?" Noelle asked, astonished.

"Yes, heaven help me, I am."

That was all Darcy would say and when she changed the subject, Noelle was sensitive enough to pretend not to notice. "Enough about that soap opera, how are things going between you two?"

"Pretty good."

"Just pretty good?" Darcy wouldn't let her off that easily. "Come on, I want a full cowboy update."

"I see Brody whenever he's in town. But he's really busy right now, it's the height of the summer racing season."

"And as usual, you're the soul of understanding."

"Actually, it works out fine. Between the boys and all the extra work I've been doing here, I'd be too tired for anything hot and heavy. His absences help me keep things in perspective and I need that."

"So what's your game plan, Chandler?" Darcy teased. "The busier you are the less danger there is of anything too serious developing?"

That was another thing Noelle admired about Darcy. Her perceptiveness. "Something like that," she admitted. "But it backfired on me. I found out it's true what they say about absence making the heart grow fonder," she admitted with a smile. Brody's sporadic visits made Noelle's long, hard days brighter.

Theirs was a hit-or-miss courtship at best. Noelle wasn't sure if it could even be called that, but she didn't have a better term. The problem was courtship implied a given resolution—namely matrimony—and she had no idea where their relationship was headed. The attraction they shared was too steamy for friendship and too well chaperoned to evolve into more.

"And?" Darcy prompted.

Noelle compared her and Brody's situation to an old movie she'd once seen. "It was set in Ireland. This courting couple, John Wayne and Maureen O'Hara if memory serves, had to ride in a special cart driven by a matchmaker. They sat on opposite sides, facing in opposite directions, their backs separated by at least a foot. And they were expected to get to know each other under those circumstances."

"You and your old movies," Darcy teased. "What's that got to do with you and Brody?"

"It pretty much sums up the time we spend together. Maybe we don't have a wizened Barry Fitzgerald over-seeing our every move, but Dusty and Danny do an admirable job of filling his shoes. In both the matchmaking and chaperoning departments.''

Since their date at Cowboy's Noelle had come to expect the unexpected from Brody. He followed a timetable all his own, one that was totally incomprehensible to normal nine-to-fivers like herself. She worried that he might not be eating right, and she cooked for him when he was home.

''Since he and the boys get along so well, entertainment is limited to activities guaranteed to elevate kinetic levels in four-year-olds. We eat in noisy pizza parlors with singing mechanical gorillas instead of in romantic French restaurants with strolling troubadors. And when we go to the movies, we forgo love stories for feature-length cartoons.''

Darcy gulped down the rest of her sandwich before they returned to work. ''I've heard of matches made in heaven, but this one sounds more like it was made in Disneyland.''

The next time Noelle saw Brody she expressed, casually of course, a desire to know more about what he did for a living. He offered to take her to lunch at Remington Park. That way she could see for herself how exciting quarter horse racing could be.

Although it was Sunday Mrs. Sterling was willing to sit with the boys and Noelle anticipated a whole afternoon alone with the man she'd come to think of as her very own cowboy.

She'd never been to the racetrack before, so when they arrived Brody gave her a short tour of the luxurious facilities. ''Oklahoma is to quarter horses what Kentucky is to Thoroughbreds,'' he explained as he directed her up the escalator.

"So it's true that Oklahoma is the quarter horse capital of the world?" Noelle asked. "I thought it was just hype from the tourism department."

"It's true all right. Remington hosts Thoroughbred meets in the spring and fall," he explained. "But the summer belongs to the quarter horse."

All of Noelle's preconceived notions about racetracks dissolved as Brody showed her around. Remington Park, encompassing over three hundred acres landscaped with thousands of shrubs and trees, was an overwhelming sight in itself.

But most imposing of all was the glass-enclosed, climate-controlled stadium that presented panoramic views of the track from each of four levels. Two giant screens and over three hundred video monitors promoted the high tech excitement that mounted as post time drew near.

A glass tunnel through the stadium allowed fans to watch every step of the Parade to Post and the beautifully landscaped Paddock Gardens amphitheater provided the setting for prerace pageantry. When Noelle admired the predominately red flowering plants Brody told her the periwinkles, begonias, salvias and vincas were all grown in an on-the-grounds greenhouse.

The Infield Park was a place for families to have fun since no one under eighteen was allowed access to the rest of the facilities.

Noelle took in the sights with a mixture of awe and delight. "I had no idea it was so big. Or so clean! How do they keep a four-story wall of glass so shiny?"

Brody shrugged. "Lots of elbow grease and window cleaner, I guess."

"Where are we going now?" she asked as he led her back on to the escalator.

"I thought we'd go up and find our table. There's twenty-four places to eat here, but the Silks Clubhouse Restaurant is my favorite."

They went up to the third level and as Noelle observed the well-dressed people around her, she was glad she'd worn her best white suit. She made a striking contrast to Brody who was dressed in desperado black—black Western-cut suit, black hat, black boots. Even his shirt was black.

They were seated near the finish line at a linen-covered table, complete with fresh flowers, by a waiter who seemed well acquainted with Brody.

"Nice to have you back, Mr. Sawyer," the young man said deferentially as he handed them leather-bound menus. "Can I bring you and the lady something to drink?"

They ordered iced tea and when the waiter left, Noelle turned to Brody. "I'm impressed. I don't know where I got the idea that racetracks were a hang-out for cigar-smoking, hot dog-noshing, dyed-in-the-wool gamblers."

Brody was glad her misconceptions had been shattered and even happier that she was enjoying herself while learning more about his business. That was one of the reasons he'd brought her here. The other, more important one, was so that he could tell her all about Cimarron and himself.

Today was true confession time, better late than never. But first, they'd eat. There was nothing like a little shrimp scampi to put a person in a receptive mood.

When she wouldn't cease to be amazed, he told her, "You should see the Penthouse level. Everything's grade-A plush up there—the club, the restaurant and the suites that are leased year around by businesses and the high rollers.''

"I wouldn't exactly call this slumming," she mused with a gesture at the gleaming silver and sparkling crystal on the table. She grimaced when she saw the prices on the menu. Could Brody afford to spend so much just to impress her?

He saw her frowning at the menu and teased, "Order whatever you want, but the shrimp is great."

"If you're sure?" she asked hesitantly.

"I'm sure. Do you think I'm some kind of penniless bum or something?"

The way she flushed, Brody knew he'd struck a nerve. "Of course not. It just seems like a lot to eat for lunch is all," she said lamely.

The waiter returned with their drinks, and Brody took the decision away from her by ordering for both of them. When they were alone he said, "I know you must have a lot of questions. Why don't you ask them and I'll try to give you some answers?"

Noelle read an announcement on one of the large screens. "What's post time?"

"That's when the race starts. You've got ten minutes, so if you want to make a wager, you should do it before the lines form at the windows."

She shook her head. "Not me. I'm not going to help them pay for this expensive building."

Brody laughed. "This isn't Las Vegas, you're not betting against the house. Remington Park has no stake in who wins. The term pari-mutuel comes from the French. 'Pari,' among. 'Mutuel,' ourselves. Wagering against ourselves."

"Are you saying the track doesn't get any of the money wagered?"

"Out of each dollar bet, the winning bettors get eighty-two cents and the other eighteen is divided up for the track, the state and the purse."

"Whose purse?" she asked skeptically.

"The purse is the money awarded to the winners of the race."

"Well, I don't know much about it, so I think I'll pass." But when she opened up the daily program she saw that in the first race, horse number four was a gray two-year-old gelding named Dusty Dan.

"Dusty and Danny are four. That's just too much of a coincidence," she said. "Maybe I should bet on him."

"The odds are twenty to one," Brody cautioned as he scanned the tote board. "He doesn't have a record of early leads or top finishing positions. He's a long shot. That means the odds are against him. I never pick a long shot unless it's one of my horses and I know what he can do."

"I know," she said. "I'll just bet on him for fun. For the boys."

"I've heard of stranger reasons for picking a horse. Some people look for a pretty animal that holds up his tail. Others bet on black horses wearing red blankets. One woman I know goes by how cute the jockey is, so I guess your reasoning is as sound as any."

He took her up a short flight of steps and showed her how to place her bet at the window. Ever conservative, she wagered two dollars on number four to win. As they stepped away Brody was whistling, "Hey, Big Spender," under his breath.

Back at their table he gave her some background information as they watched the horses parade to the post. "There are three types of races in quarter horse racing," he explained. "Short sprints, long sprints, and hooks which make one turn around the track. Short-distance horses are stockier in build, while long-distance horses are taller and lankier.''

"The only race I've ever seen is the Kentucky Derby on television,'' she admitted. "These horses don't look like Thoroughbreds.''

"That's a good observation. Quarter horses must have the power to make explosive starts and to run full-throttle down the straightaway. That power comes from a compact, heavily muscled body. They're especially strong through the buttock, thigh and gaskin areas.''

"I know what the first two are, but what on earth is a gaskin?''

He chuckled. Maybe he didn't know much about books and plays, but he knew horses. "The gaskin is the mid hind-leg area. The strength in its hindquarter accounts for the quickness of the start and the ability to sustain a top speed in races as short as two hundred and twenty yards or as long as one thousand yards.''

"A quick start is important then?''

"It's essential. Quarter horses lunge from the gate, reaching top speed after the first stride and they run the short distance full out. There's no competing for position before the jockey asks his horse to take the lead. From the instant the gate opens until the finish, the horse has to give it all he's got. A good one has to be aggressive, but he also has to have the will to win.

"The all-out speed makes quarter horses the fastest breed in racing. They can carry one hundred and twenty pounds of rider and tack at speeds in excess of fifty-five miles an hour. They can cover a quarter mile in less than twenty-two seconds from a standing start. So if you blink, you might miss it.''

Noelle spotted Dusty Dan on the track below. "How does he look to you?" she asked anxiously, surprised to learn that she was not immune to all the excitement, after all.

"Not bad," he responded noncommittally. "He carries his head high and he seems alert. He looks calm and ready to run."

"Is that good?"

"Sure. A nervous horse washes out. We say he runs the race in the paddock. You don't want a horse to expend so much energy before the race that he has nothing left. Also, your horse has a smooth, even stride. That means he's not favoring a sore leg."

"That's encouraging," she remarked dryly.

"Hey, it's just a sport."

At that moment the alerting notes of the herald trumpet sounded, the post-time bell clanged and the track announcer called out the magic words: "And they're off!"

By the time Noelle located the starting gate, which was moved from race to race, it was all over. "Well, heck!" she complained with a frustrated sigh. "I didn't see a thing."

The announcer came back on. "The winner is horse number four. Dusty Dan ridden by..."

But she didn't hear the rest. She was too busy jumping up and down and hugging Brody. "I won! I won!"

"It was just a two-dollar bet," he teased. "You act like you just won back the homestead from black-hearted Harry."

"I know, but it's so exciting."

"Aren't you going upstairs to collect your winnings?"

"My winnings?" she asked, wide-eyed. "How much?"

"Well, Miss Moneybags, I'd say you've got about forty dollars coming to you."

While waiting for lunch to be served, Noelle used her windfall to bet on a few more races but her beginner's luck didn't hold out. She promptly forswore wagering, preferring instead to pick her favorites informally.

While she devoured the delicious shrimp scampi, Brody fed her some of the history of the industry, as well. It soon became clear that horses were his raison d'être. His enthusiasm was so great that she had to wonder if maybe he wasn't like those nervous horses. Did he expend so much energy and emotion in his work that he didn't have any left over for anything else?

"Quarter horses were originally bred for the qualities needed in frontier ranching, basically early speed and levelheadedness," he told her. "Match racing was the favorite sport in those days, so few early races were started at gates. If a horse was too excitable, he could never be a successful racehorse, any more than he could be a good cow horse."

"Now that gates are used, is it any different?" Noelle asked.

"Levelheadedness isn't the major concern to racehorse breeders that it once was. Nowadays, they breed for speed alone. But Dub Roberts is from the old school. He says if breeders aren't careful, they'll lose the other basic quarter horse characteristic: cow sense. Dub taught me that cow sense and a quiet disposition go hand in hand and I look for that in horses I train. Lose one, Dub says, and you lose the other. Lose them both, and you lose the quarter horse."

While they ate, several people, both men and women, stopped by to speak to Brody and Noelle became aware that he was a very popular man at Remington Park. After their plates were cleared away, she folded her arms on the table and leaned toward him.

"Brody, what is it that you do exactly?" she asked earnestly. "If you don't mind me asking."

"Not at all. That's one reason I brought you here today. It seems like when we're together, there's so many distractions, we don't get much talking done."

"Well, two distractions that I can think of, right off hand," she pointed out with a smile.

Over sinfully rich ice cream parfaits, Brody answered all her questions. "Riley and I own a hundred and sixty acres ten miles east of here. We established Cimarron Racing Stables over ten years ago. It's taken a lot of hard work, but it's now one of the best on the circuit. My dream is that some day it will be *the* best."

"You own your own place?" she asked. "But I thought..."

"I know what you thought, Noelle, and I'm sorry I misrepresented myself. But when we first met, I didn't want you to think I was bragging or trying to impress you, so I didn't say anything about Cimarron. Later, it just didn't seem that important."

"I take it Cimarron is something to brag about, then."

"We're pretty proud of it. Dub helped us get started but Riley and I have built the stables up from almost nothing. When we bought the property, there were a couple of tumbledown sheds, a barn with walls you could toss a cat through and a small frame house. Because of Dub's connections, a few owners were willing to take a chance on us and we worked our way up from there."

He continued, "Word of mouth is important in this business. Owning racehorses is expensive, so those owners who can afford to hire trainers are usually wealthy and influential. If they put in a good word for you in the right circles, it helps.''

She sat quietly as she tried to take in everything he'd said. She thought about the well-dressed people who treated him with such deference and realized that he must be quite a success in his chosen field. ''Your track record didn't hurt, did it?''

''Now that you mention it, no,'' he admitted modestly. ''I've trained the last two All-American Futurity winners. Hope to do it again this year.''

When she didn't say anything, he asked, ''Does it make a difference, Noelle? Because as much as I'd like to be poor for you, I have this thing about winning. And winning trainers are not poor.''

She looked up and saw him watching her expectantly as he chewed nervously on a wooden toothpick. ''You big dummy,'' she said in exasperated reproach. ''I thought you pitched hay and shoveled manure.''

''If it makes you feel any better, I've done plenty of both. When Riley and I started out, we had to do everything ourselves. Now we've got about ten hands to help out, but there never seems to be enough time to do all the work that needs to be done. Early on, we got in the habit of working twenty-hour days, so maybe that's why I have so much trouble letting go of work. Are you mad at me?''

''How can I be mad at you for being successful? Besides, I was never interested in your bank account.''

''Well, you sure couldn't be interested in my mind.'' He leaned across the table. ''So what are you interested in, lady? My body?''

Once again she was astonished at the way her senses reacted to him. She felt flushed and needy and dangerously close to proclaiming her true feelings. Instead she picked up her spoon and told him airly, "Right now, all I'm interested in is my black forest sundae."

Brody grinned around the toothpick and relaxed in his chair. He was relieved his confession had been so well-received. But why not? She was one hell of an understanding woman. "Noelle."

"Yes?"

"I know you don't want to bet anymore, but would you like to do some high-stakes wagering, just between the two of us?" His hazel eyes turned dark.

"High stakes?" she asked warily.

"Yeah. See, here's how it works. You pick a horse and if it wins, I owe you a kiss. I pick a horse and if it wins, you owe me one. We can collect later. After the boys go to sleep." And in case she didn't get his drift he added with a raised brow, "When we're alone."

"What if neither one of our horses win?"

"Why, then we both get a consolation prize."

His grin leavened her spirits. Leave it to Brody to clear the air and create a no-lose contest. "You're on, cowboy."

After three more races Brody stood. "Let's take a walk down to the track level. I have a filly in this race and she's looking good today."

"Which one?"

"Number six, Mama's Cookin'."

Once they reached the paddock area Brody left Noelle at the fence while he saw to the saddling of his horse and spoke to the jockey. He rejoined her for the thunderous start of the three-hundred-yard sprint. The finish was incredibly close, as it often was in quarter horse racing, but even to Noelle's untrained eye the winner was undeniably number six.

Caught up in the excitement she flung her arms about Brody's neck. He lifted her, swinging her around and around and then setting her back on her feet, he grabbed her hand. "Let's go."

"Where to?" she cried as they dodged their way through the milling crowd.

"Where we belong," he said as he looked deeply into her eyes. "The winner's circle."

They hung around for a few more races and Noelle gathered as much reading material as possible from the information booths. She enjoyed the day immensely and being at Brody's side while he was celebrated by peers and fans alike only added to her pleasure.

That night when the twins were snug in their beds, Brody and Noelle settled the day's wagers.

With interest.

Chapter Eight

They continued to see each other, and the uncertain quality of their time together made it more precious to both of them. When Brody was away he called almost every night. One evening as Noelle settled down with a book she'd been saving for a lonely night, the phone rang. Before she could answer a sexy voice said, "Hi, honey. It's the zoo pervert."

She laughed. "What if you'd dialed the wrong number? It could happen, you know."

"Only to lucky guys who live right and don't cheat on their taxes." Brody tried to keep his tone light, but he missed her more than he ever thought he could miss anyone.

Talking on the phone just wasn't enough. He wanted to see her. In his physical state, even seeing her might not be enough. "I'll be in Oklahoma tomorrow, can you go out?"

"I wasn't expecting you until next week and I promised the boys we'd cook hamburgers outside. Why don't you join us."

"You're not running a soup kitchen for transient males, Mrs. Chandler. I eat at your house too much. It's time I treated you."

"Nonsense. You've taken us to movies and the miniature golf course and the pizza joint. Besides, you have the added expense of traveling, not to mention all these telephone calls. A few puny hamburgers is the least I can do."

"I belong to a mileage club at the airline." Brody was amused by Noelle's frugal mind set. Even now that she knew he was financially solvent, she still worried about money—probably because with two kids to raise she had to watch every penny of her income. It made him really mad when he thought about Steven Chandler and the way he'd made things hard for her.

Brody had been tempted more than once to offer her money, especially when the item in question was something frivolous that the boys wanted. But he knew better. Noelle would never take that kind of help from him. But there was more than one way to skin a possum and he'd developed the habit of listening to both little boys' yearnings and surprising them with gifts on his trips home.

Noelle always protested that he was spoiling them but by then they had the wrappings ripped off and it was too late. Besides, he enjoyed making them happy and if bringing them trinkets spoiled them, he was sorry. He'd never had anyone to spoil before and he liked the feeling it gave him.

In fact, his whole relationship with Noelle and her children was a new experience for him and he'd started thinking about what it would be like to share the laughing and loving and tears of family life on a daily basis.

He often wondered if he could handle it and worried that his hard-scrabble childhood might have handicapped him emotionally. He hadn't had much nurturing or affection in his formative years and he found it incredibly overwhelming when Dusty and Danny looked to him for those things.

He tried to treat them as he wished his father had treated him and they responded with innocent adoration.

Brody's feelings for Noelle could not be dealt with so easily. His early life in the dirt hills of eastern Oklahoma had provided little in the way of joy or beauty and now, because of Noelle, he had so much of both. He'd never known anyone so special, and sometimes he was afraid he didn't deserve her.

Some of his earliest memories revolved around his father telling him how worthless he was—how things would be different if he and Riley weren't around. So Brody lay awake nights, worrying that someday Noelle would come to realize how unlovable he was and then she'd be gone.

He could try to prove himself worthy, wasn't that what he'd been doing all his life? But work was the only thing he knew. He'd figured out early that the key to success was hard work. So he'd focused on that, ignoring everything else in the hopes that someday—if he worked hard enough to deserve it—someone might love him.

And now that it appeared someone could love him, he was scared to death. Not that he was ready to admit it, but he was dangerously close to losing his heart to the two little rascals and their pretty mother. His first impulse was to run away from the feelings that shook him, but something wouldn't let him do that.

He suddenly realized he'd only been half listening as Noelle recounted some of the boys' latest antics and put in, "Dusty and Danny and I will do all the cooking and cleaning up. Deal?"

"All right, but I should warn you that the only thing the boys know how to make is a mess."

"We'll learn together."

"Now wait just a darn minute, cowboy."

"I was teasing."

"I'm glad you're cooking outside, I don't think I should trust you in my kitchen." What she was really afraid of trusting him with was her heart.

"Not to worry, I know my way around charcoal briquets. And I'm no slouch in the kitchen, either."

"If you know so much, what are parsley, sage, rosemary and thyme?"

"A hit song from the sixties?" Brody guessed.

She laughed. "Just as I thought."

"Okay, they're herbs. I knew it all the time. So, take it from me, I'm pretty damn good in the kitchen." Then in a tone loaded with innuendo, he said "And I ain't too shabby in a few other rooms, either."

"I'll just bet you aren't," she agreed in a voice made breathless by the image he evoked. "But can you cook?"

When Brody arrived at Noelle's house the next day, he noticed a difference in her and the boys. She allowed him to greet her with an easy hug and kiss on the cheek, but her general attitude seemed preoccupied and detached.

Although the twins thanked him for the cowboy hats he brought them, they did so without the usual yipping and skipping. He had to work extra hard for every halfhearted giggle he wrangled out of them.

He knew something was troubling all of them, but since Noelle offered no information he was hesitant to pry. Later, as he stood on her small patio, flipping burgers and listening to crickets chirp, he tried to figure out what he'd done wrong.

Noelle sat in a webbed lawn chair and watched Brody working at the grill. Normally, she enjoyed this time of day when the evening shadows stretched across the flower beds she'd planted with marigolds and zinnias. Blossoms from a rose of sharon bush floated in the water of a bird bath in the corner and beneath it sat a whimsically winking green frog that she'd bought on impulse because it reminded the boys of their favorite character in the Frog and Toad stories.

She always smiled when she saw that silly frog, but today he'd lost his magic. Damn, Steve, anyway.

"We brung out all the stuff," Dusty told Brody in a strangely subdued voice.

"Whaddya want us to do now, Brody?" Danny's eyes lacked their usual sparkle.

"We can't do much until the meat cooks." He closed the lid on the grill and nodded at the gaily striped swing set. "Why don't we get in some swinging while we wait."

Danny shrugged and glanced at his mother who was staring pensively at a butterfly fluttering among the marigolds. "I don't feel like swingin' right now."

Dusty's gaze followed his brother's. "Me, neither."

The boys seemed as concerned about Noelle as he was. "Then how about we keep your momma company?"

They agreed and Brody sat in the chair next to hers while both boys sat quietly at her feet instead of arguing about who would sit in his lap.

"Was it something I said?" he asked.

She looked at him as if she'd forgotten all about him. "What?"

He repeated his question, then gestured at the boys. "Did I do something wrong?"

"Oh, no. The boys have had a bad day, is all."

"Anything I can fix?" If he could, he'd bundle up their problems and throw them down a well.

"No."

"I guess you don't owe me any explanations. It's enough to know I'm not responsible for the mood. I was beginning to think they didn't like me anymore."

"It's nothing like that, I'll tell you about it later." She gave him a little-pitchers-have-big-ears look.

Brody wished he knew more about children and the things that made them happy. He'd do anything to see the two little imps smile again.

Remembering how he and Riley had always worked out their frustrations in friendly wrestling, Brody pulled off his boots and flopped down in the sweet-smelling grass. "Bet you boys don't do much wrestling," he challenged.

Dusty and Danny glanced at each other, then at their mother. She encouraged them with a smile and Dusty was the first to respond. "Sure we do, it's pretty fun."

"But we can't do it in the house," Danny qualified.

"Then isn't it lucky we just happen to be outside?" Brody lurched with a growl, grabbing a boy in each arm, and pulled them down on top of him. He tickled, nuzzled and rolled on the ground until both were squealing with delight.

By the time Noelle remembered to check on their dinner, smoke was roiling out of the grill and the burgers were an unappetizing shade of black. Noelle hoped the neighbors wouldn't notice and she clanged the spatula against the grill and called, "Come and get it, cowboys!"

Brody scooped a boy under each arm and deposited them on a bench at the picnic table. "We'll play some more after dinner," he told them when they complained.

"We wanna play now." Dusty swung his legs and folded his little arms across his chest in a defiant gesture.

"Yeah," Danny agreed as he assumed his brother's pose. "What if you forget?"

Brody put on a face filled with mock indignation. "Hey, pardners, a deal's a deal. I won't forget. Soon as we clear away our mess, we'll play again." It wasn't something he'd done many times in his life but Brody added, "I promise."

Dusty tugged on his hand. "Is that a pretend promise like Daddy makes?"

"Or a real promise like Momma makes?" Danny asked.

He glanced at Noelle who was slathering mustard on a bun. She paused, a worried look in her eyes.

So that's what this was all about. Steve Chandler had reneged on something else. His heart went out to the small boys whose innocent blue eyes were filled with reluctant distrust. He knew what they were feeling. The first nine years of his own life were based on one broken promise after another.

"I don't believe in pretend promises," he told them seriously. "So if I ever promise you guys or your momma anything, you can count on me to keep it."

"Really real?" Dusty asked.

"Really real," Brody confirmed. "Cowboy's honor."

Noelle didn't realize she was holding her breath until it escaped in a rush. "Now that that's all settled, let's eat. I'm starving."

Dusty lifted his bun and flicked at the burger with distaste. "Mine's all black and yucky on one side."

"So's mine," Danny put in. "They're not supposed to be black, are they?"

Noelle was about to remind them that the very well-done cuisine was a result of a cook who was too busy rolling in the grass to tend to his work when Brody saved the day.

"These are ranch-style burgers," he improvised in an encouraging voice.

"Really?" The boys looked doubtfully from their hero to their plates.

"Well, sure. Out on the range the cowboys always eat their buffalo burgers black. It adds flavor. We even have a saying about it. 'When it's smokin', it's cookin.' When it's black it's done."

The boys giggled and attacked their charred burgers with new gusto. Noting the happy twinkle in their eyes, Brody congratulated himself on his unexpected advancement in child psychology. Again he marveled at how little it took to brighten their world, and how much he enjoyed being the one to do it.

Noelle gave him a grateful look before warning, "Eat carefully, guys, we don't want any premature tooth loss."

Brody snapped off a piece of black crust, popped it into his mouth and chewed. "M-m-m-m," he feigned an ecstasy he didn't feel. "They aren't too hard to chew. They only *look* and *taste* like charcoal briquets." He stretched to grab the catsup and shook out an excessive amount. "A little extra catsup will take care of that."

When the meal was over both Dusty and Danny claimed Brody's were the best charcoal briquets they'd ever eaten. While he put things away and Noelle sat at the kitchen table to keep him company, the boys fetched in the food and dishes.

"I know you probably don't believe this, but I really can cook," he told her.

"That line's right up there with *Of course I'll still respect you in the morning*, *Your check's in the mail*, and my all-time favorite, *One size fits all*."

He sauntered over to the table, took her hand, and pulled her from the chair. He bent her back in a gesture that was right out of *The Sheik* and with his lips hovering over hers said with mock ferocity, "Admit it, lady. Tell me I'm good in the kitchen."

He kissed her briefly and even though the caress was meant to tease, it felt as if crazed butterflies swarmed in her stomach. "Okay, okay." She shoved away from him when she heard the screen door slam. "You're good in the kitchen. But as I said last night that doesn't make you a cook."

"Then I'll prove it to you tomorrow night. The boys and I will fix you a special dinner and have it ready when you come home from work."

"Awright!" Dusty and Danny raced into the kitchen and nearly dropped the big jar of pickles they carried.

"The boys are at the day-care center until I pick them up after work," she reminded him.

"Call the center and tell them I'll get the twins early. We'll do the shopping, come home and have it ready by the time you get here."

"Yeah," Dusty agreed.

"Can we? Can we?" Danny jumped up and down in place.

Noelle looked into their happy little faces. How could she deny them this small thing when they'd already lost so much? "Okay, but you'd better scoot outside and get the rest of the leftovers, it'll be dark soon."

"I'm sorry," he said, as soon as the boys raced out, banging the screen door again.

"For what?"

"I didn't realize until it was too late that I put you in an awkward position. I should have waited until we were alone to ask."

She looked at him thoughtfully. "I think maybe you knew exactly what you were doing, Brody Sawyer."

He returned her grin. "Maybe I did, at that."

When kitchen duty was over, Brody and the boys got down to some serious wrestling and tickling. They were having so much fun that Noelle hated to break it up. But if Dusty and Danny got overstimulated this time of night, it would be hours before they would settle down to sleep.

"Time to take your baths and get ready for bed."

"Aw, heck." Dusty supplemented his complaint with the traditional aw-heck arm swing.

"Just a little longer?" Danny wheedled.

"You heard your momma," Brody said with a exaggerated cowpoke twang. "It's round-up time on the range so I reckon I better herd all you little dogies into the corral."

The boys ran shrieking down the hall ahead of him as he twirled an invisible lasso.

When Noelle tried to follow them into the bathroom, Brody shut the door between them. "No girls allowed," he pronounced playfully. "I'll scrub down these ornery critters."

"Are you sure you know what you're getting into?"

"I think I can figure it out," he said, rolling up his sleeves.

Noelle listened outside the door for a moment. Danny won the coin toss and so got to pour in the bubble bath. Dusty showed Brody where the linens were kept and explained that they were supposed to wash everything. And use soap. After that, all she heard was a lot of splashing. And a few muted strains of "Git Along, Little Dogies."

When they emerged half an hour later, the boys were spiffed, brushed, slicked down and dressed in matching cowboy-motif pajamas, gifts from New Mexico. Brody's mussed hair and water-spotted clothing were evidence of his first valiant attempt at what Darcy claimed should be an endurance test at the Olympics: twin washing.

Noelle smiled at their fresh scrubbed faces and sniffed the lingering scent of bubble bath. Then she made a big ceremony of walking around each child, pretending to inspect him from head to toe. "You get a perfect ten, Sawyer."

"Now what're we gonna do?" Dusty wanted to know.

Thinking she might try one of Brody's tactics, Noelle said, "Head for the bunkhouse, pardners."

"Can we have a story first?" Dusty asked.

"Sure," Noelle told him. "Pick out a book and hurry back." Story reading was one of their nightly routines.

"Not a book," Danny objected. "We want Brody to *tell* us story. About horses."

"And cowboys," Dusty put in.

Brody agreed and the twins snuggled down between him and their mother. He wasn't sure how it had happened, or when, but he could now tell them apart.

He squinted down into Dusty's upturned face. "Are you Dusty or Ralph," he asked, just to show off.

"Dusty." Giggle, giggle.

"Then you," he pointed to Danny, "must be Ralph."

"Naw, I'm Danny." Giggle, giggle.

He peered into their faces. "You guys are so clean I didn't recognize you." He turned to Noelle. "Did you?"

"Nope. Until they told us I thought they were just a couple of strays who wandered in here off the range."

The boys were nearly asleep by the time Brody finished his Pecos Bill story and he and Noelle carried them to their little beds. While she fetched cups of water, he pulled the covers up to Dusty's chin.

The boy hugged him fiercely around the neck. "Nighty-night, Brody."

The same thing happened when he leaned over Danny.

Brody kissed each boy on the cheek and smoothed back the fine, blond hair that had fallen into their eyes. He recalled bedtimes from his own childhood. After his mother died, there had been no stories, no kisses, no nighty-nights.

Many nights they were left alone in the tumbledown house at the end of a lonely country road while their father drove into town for liquor and women. Brody would huddle with Riley under the unwashed sheets and tell his little brother that there was nothing to be scared of. Didn't he have Brody to protect him?

But that wasn't exactly true and they both knew it. They were wise to fear Joe Sawyer. Brody, who hadn't even started school yet, was a pretty puny guardian and Riley had been younger than the twins then.

Watching the twins' innocent little faces as they settled down to sleep, Brody was struck by how small and helpless they were, how much in need of a man's protection. Had he ever been that innocent? That helpless? How had he managed to take care of himself, much less Riley?

Noelle came back with the requested water and the boys took sleepy sips before flopping back down on their pillows. Brody switched off the light and forced down the lump in his throat. "See you tomorrow, guys."

"Promise?" someone asked drowsily.

"Promise."

In the living room he helped Noelle gather up tiny cars and plastic dinosaurs and green army guys. "They're good kids."

"What do you mean?" She looked up with a grin. "They're wonderful kids."

"That they are."

"You don't think they're too wimpy, do you?"

"Wimpy?" he said incredulously. "Of course not, why would you ask such a thing?"

"Steve says I'm stifling them, turning them into weaklings."

Brody was quiet a moment as he recalled harsher names. "What kind of man would say something like that about his own children? I think you've done a great job. And you've done it alone, no thanks to him."

"That's what I told him. He was just angry about the papers he'd received from my lawyer. We were supposed to go to court next week."

"Supposed to? Noelle, you haven't let him talk you out of suing, have you?"

"Oh, it's nothing like that. He took matters in his own hands and defected." Noelle finished tidying up and led Brody to the sofa. As she settled down beside him, she felt close to tears and got angry at Steve all over again for that.

"What's he done now?" Brody asked gently, knowing Steve had been responsible for the boys' earlier unhappiness, as well as Noelle's.

"I got a letter from him today with a lot of pretty, foreign stamps. It started out, 'Guess what? You'll prob-

ably be surprised to know I'm in Venezuela.' Yeah, big
surprise, all right."

"You mean he just up and left the country."

"That's the way he deals with things. He runs away."

"But why South America?"

"Something to do with an oil boom. He wrote that he
has a chance to quadruple his investment of fifty thousand dollars. Fifty thousand, mind you! Not too bad for
a man who can't afford to pay child support. It's just like
him to scrounge around and rake up a fortune to go off
chasing another dream." Her contempt was obvious.

"I don't condone what he's done, but what if it happens? What if he quadruples the money?"

"You've got to be kidding. I stopped living on 'what
ifs' a long time ago. I refuse to let the boys keep on hoping. The reason they were so down today was because I
had to tell them that it would be a long time before they
would see their father again."

Her resentment toward Steve no longer filled her with
strong feelings. She didn't care anymore. Not for herself. But she hated what his abandonment would mean to
Dusty and Danny. She hurt for them because some day
they would be old enough to understand that their father didn't love them enough to be a part of their lives.
She could only hope that when that time came, she'd be
able to help them through it.

Brody sat quietly, seething with anger. He knew how
it felt to be sold out and hated a man he'd never met for
doing that to Dusty and Danny. Joe Sawyer had traded
his sons for cold, hard cash. Steve Chandler wasn't so
different. "How'd they take the news?"

"They didn't bat an eye. That's what I feel so bad
about. I don't want them to resign themselves to such

treatment. It's not their fault, and it's not mine, but I can't tell you how guilty I feel."

Brody drew her into his arms. "You have nothing to feel guilty about. You've done your part. You give them enough love for ten kids."

She rested her head on his shoulder and drew courage from his strength. She loved Brody and she couldn't tell him. Whoever had hurt him, had done such a thorough job that he wouldn't let himself be loved.

When they were alone in her small house, isolated from the outside, he fit into her world like the long missing piece of a puzzle. But he had his own life, one that she wasn't sure could include her and her children. And he'd given her no indication that he wanted to become a permanent part of hers.

When she touched his shirtfront, she found it still slightly damp from the boys' bath. He'd been so cute with them tonight. They needed a good man in their lives, a strong, hard-working man they could pattern their own lives after.

Brody was such a man. She was right to worry that he was becoming too important to her and the boys.

Much too important.

Brody stroked Noelle's hair and felt some of the tension leave her body even as it mounted in his own. He wanted her so much. He wanted to be her lover, her friend. Her protector. Her knight. But he couldn't give her what she wanted. As much as he cared for her, he couldn't be the kind of man she needed. He just wasn't cut out for domestic bliss.

"Do you remember that first night I came over here?" he asked softly.

"I'll never forget it. We were practically strangers, yet you figured out that I needed a hug and when you held me, I felt better."

"I think we both need a hug tonight."

"I was hoping you'd think that," she whispered as they fell against each other. She sighed, her whole being filled with wanting. It would be so easy to be swept away by him, to give herself up to the magic that made her forget all about reality.

Inside these snug walls nothing else existed and she longed for the release she would find in Brody's arms. For the affirmation that she needed so badly.

But she had children to think of. And the future. She'd learned her lesson with Steve. The only person she could count on was herself. The only person Dusty and Danny could count on was their momma.

Brody was good and gentle and kind. But he was a long shot. So was love. Smart women didn't wager their hearts on long shots.

She tried to keep those thoughts fixed firmly in her mind, but Brody kissed her and the magic began again. She sighed and he gave her an answering moan. Deepening the kiss with sweet urgency, he tangled his fingers in her hair and held her close.

Brody realized things could get out of hand if he didn't stop soon. When he and Noelle made love, he didn't want her to suffer any regrets. When his hand moved to the buttons on her blouse he felt her stiffen and, gently, he broke the kiss. When she looked up at him, her eyes pleaded for understanding.

"I'm not ready, Brody."

"I know, honey." He stroked her cheek.

"Are you always so understanding?"

"I try to be."

"What am I going to do with you?" she asked.

"I'm open to suggestions. What did you have in mind?"

"I don't think I should get into that line of thought."

"I have to be honest, Noelle. I want to make love to you."

"I want it too, Brody. But it would be wrong. I can't teach my children good morals if I don't possess them myself."

"I know."

"I'm just not the kind of woman who can give herself to a man without a commitment."

"I'm glad. You're also a beautiful, desirable woman and I have the same physical urges any normal man would have. I'd be lying if I said the subject won't come up again."

He kissed her and while she clung to her principles, she tried to keep the uncertainty of love and other long shots firmly in mind.

She only forgot a couple of times.

Chapter Nine

Brody sat in his truck outside Miss Muffet's Children's Center watching young children run around the playground. On the seat beside him was his scuffed leather carry-on that he had packed for the return trip to New Mexico.

Brody realized he could no longer postpone the inevitable, and he tried to figure out how to tell Dusty and Danny that their date was off. The situation would have been handled quicker by phone, but quicker was not always better.

He hated breaking his promise to the boys, but it couldn't be helped. Jim Hanks, the man he'd left in charge in Ruidoso, had called him at Remington Park first thing this morning with bad news. One of the Futurity hopefuls had crashed into a rail during a workout and the resultant leg injury was a serious one.

The track vet had suggested destroying the valuable animal, but Jim didn't want to make that decision alone, not without Brody or Riley seeing the colt first.

Not wanting to disappoint Dusty and Danny, Brody had tried to reach Riley at Cimarron. Billy Sixkiller had taken the call. "Yeah, Boss?"

"I need to talk to Riley. We got an emergency in Ruidoso and I want him to fly out there on the next plane."

"Riley ain't in fit shape to fly anywhere." Billy sounded sad, though carefully nonjudgmental. He'd been with the brothers since Cimarron was little more than a dream.

"You mean he's drunk?" Brody exploded. "It's eight o'clock in the damn morning!" His own day had started before six. When he had left for Remington he noticed Riley's truck wasn't in his driveway. He'd been impressed that his brother was up and doing so early. He'd even hoped that Riley might be trying harder, that he was out on business. And so he had been—monkey business.

"He's been on a bad all-nighter," Billy told him quietly. "Some little gal name of Darcy brought him home a while ago and I helped her put him to bed."

"He was with Darcy?"

"No. She said he broke a date with her last night and she got worried about him. Said she got her brother to help her look for him and they found him passed out in his pickup outside one of those sleazy joints downtown."

"Damn!" Brody raked a hand through his hair and fought to control his rising temper. "What time was that?"

"She said about four this morning. They took him to a diner for coffee. By the time they got here, he was wide awake, but he was still drunkern' a peach-orchard sow."

Brody slapped the wall in frustration. How had he let this happen? Darcy wasn't responsible for Riley, that was *his* job. Since he'd been six years old, Brody had always put Riley first. He'd tried to shield him from the worst of the things life had pitched their way. Where had he gone wrong?

It had all started with Candi. Brody had seen right through the money-hungry little conniver and had warned Riley that she was just out for what she could get. But trying to talk him out of something was like waving a red flag in front of a bull. Next thing Brody knew, his brother was married. And miserable.

The sham marriage had lasted five years. Five years in which Candi had done her damnedest to create a rift between the two brothers. She hadn't liked the Roberts either, even though Dub and Ruby had done everything they could to keep the peace.

When she hadn't gotten what she wanted, Candi had bailed out. It was a nasty and expensive divorce. Without so much as an I-told-you-so, Brody agreed to mortgage Cimarron so Riley could pay the ridiculous settlement Candi's attorney had demanded.

Riley was over Candi, that wasn't the problem. But he couldn't handle losing contact with her two children. Even though he'd been the only father they knew for five years, he now had no legal right to visitation. Candi was using Tyler and Jamaica as an ace in the hole, with which she bartered a few hours of visitation when she wanted more money.

Candi had never displayed an abundance of motherly instincts and Riley worried about the effect her instability might have on her kids. Brody knew that most of his problems stemmed from the feeling that he'd somehow let everyone down: Dub and Ruby, Brody and the children.

It had been two years since the divorce and instead of getting better, Riley was getting worse, if this last episode was any indication. Thanks to their Futurity wins, Cimarron was in the clear again, but emotionally Riley was a long way from operating in the black.

Not once during all those years of sacrifice and doing without had Brody ever begrudged Riley a thing. But this stunt made him madder at his brother than he had ever been. Hell, Darcy and her brother had no business poking around in that part of town. It could have been dangerous. What the hell was the matter with Riley? Didn't he ever think of anyone except himself?

Brody remembered Billy waiting patiently on the other end of the line. "Will he be all right, Billy?" His voice was filled with the exhausted resignation he felt.

"He'll prob'ly sleep the clock round. Then he's gonna have one heck of a head buster when he wakes up. But I reckon he'll live."

"I guess that's good news."

"You goin' to Ruidoso, Boss?"

"I have to. Take care of things until I get back."

Brody had hung up, checked the bag he kept packed in the truck at all times, and driven here—Miss Muffet's Children's Center.

The woman in the office told him the twins were on the playground with their class. As he stepped out into the bright sunshine, a middle-aged lady in a pink-striped smock waved at him.

"You must be Mr. Sawyer," she said, extending her hand. "I'm Mary Johnson, Dusty's and Danny's teacher. The boys have been so excited about today. It's all they've talked about."

Brody's heart sank. This wasn't going to be easy. "Where are the boys, Miss Johnson?"

She shaded her eyes with her hand and scanned the romping children. "There they are, in the fort. They dearly love playing cowboy."

Brody explained that he wouldn't be taking the boys home, after all, and then walked through the sandy lot to the wooden structure that only roughly resembled a fort. Before he could spot them among the laughing, climbing children, he heard two familiar voices shriek his name.

"Are we goin' now, Brody?" Dusty asked.

"We told all the other kids about you," Danny added.

He took the twins' hands and led them to a shady swing under a tree. "There's a problem, guys," he explained. "I have to hurry back to New Mexico because one of my horses got hurt real bad."

The bright smiles faded fast and tears sparkled in their eyes. "You mean that you're not taking us home?" Dusty cried.

"Ain't we gonna cook for Momma?" Danny echoed in the same stricken voice.

"I'm afraid not. Not this time."

"But you promised." Dusty's three little words harbored accusation, reproach and defeated acceptance all at once.

Refusing to meet his eyes, the boys scuffed their high-top sneakers in the sand and backhanded their tears.

"I knew it," Danny muttered.

"I know you're disappointed and I wouldn't consider going back on my word if it weren't an emergency. I have to go, can you understand that?" It was a lot to ask of four-year-olds, but Brody prayed silently for their forgiveness.

Dusty was the first to recover. "That's okay, Brody. We know your horse is real 'portant."

"More 'portant than dumb old cookin'," Danny said with a catch in his voice. "More 'portant than us." With that he tore across the playground toward Miss Johnson who scooped him up and soothed him.

Brody's heart tightened. He hadn't handled this very well. Now what was he going to do? He started after Danny but instead sat down in the swing. What could he say to the child that didn't sound like an excuse?

"Don't worry 'bout Danny," Dusty advised sagely. He climbed onto Brody's lap and wrapped an arm around his neck. "He'll be awright. Momma says he's the 'motional one in the fambly."

Brody smiled at the sweet-faced child, grateful for what amounted to an absolution. "You understand, don't you, Dusty?"

"Oh, sure I do. I'm glad you come'd to tell us, Brody."

"So am I, pardner," Brody stood and hefted Dusty up into his arms. "Can I have a hug?"

Dusty smiled. "Sure can."

Brody felt a tug on his jeans and looked down. Danny stared up at him, looking semicomposed but still anxious. "I'm sorry, Brody."

"No problem, buddy." He picked up Danny and carried both boys over to Miss Johnson where he said goodbye. He was walking toward his truck when he heard a small voice call his name.

He turned around and saw the twins peering through the chain-link fence.

"Yeah, guys?"

"Horses ain't more 'portant to you than us, are they?" Danny wanted to know.

"Of course not."

His answer had been automatic, but as he drove to the airport he had time to really think about the question. How did he reconcile the demands of his profession with his personal life? If his relationship with Noelle continued to progress at the rate it had been going for the past few months, would the day eventually come when he'd have to make a choice?

If that happened, what would his choice be? Love and marriage were a fearsome responsibility, and when you added in the fragile feelings of two little kids, it was not only scary, it was overwhelming. Did he know what he was doing?

By the time Brody picked up his ticket and checked in, he barely had time to call Noelle. Quickly explaining the emergency, he told her he'd already seen the boys.

"They were disappointed, but I think they understood."

"Good," she said crisply. It had started. She should have known things were too good to be true.

"What's wrong?" he asked with a heavy sigh.

"Nothing. Go and do what you have to do."

"You sound like you don't understand."

"I do. And I appreciate you taking the time to stop by and explain things to the boys." Noelle really was grateful for that. Now she had to be firm and not let Brody talk her out of feelings she knew she was entitled to.

"So why do I get the feeling you're scratching my name off your list even as we speak?"

"Don't you have a plane to catch?"

"Yes, but I can't go until I know you aren't mad."

"I don't know what I am, Brody, but it's not mad. I knew this kind of thing would happen. You're a busy man and you've gone out of your way to see me and the boys this summer. I just don't know if it'll work."

"If what will work, Noelle?" Brody checked his watch and saw that he had only a few minutes before boarding. He couldn't afford to let that plane take off without him.

"I don't think this is the time to go into it, but since you brought it up, I have to tell you that this kind of disappointment is hard on Dusty and Danny. Even if I was willing to play second fiddle to a bunch of racehorses, I don't think I could let my boys do that. They get enough broken promises from their father."

"God, Noelle! That's not fair and you know it."

"Maybe not. But that's the way it is."

Before Brody could reply, his flight was called. "Listen, Noelle. I have to go now. But we can talk about this when I get home."

"I'm not sure it would do any good. I know where you stand and you know where I stand."

This wasn't working out and Brody didn't know what to do. In truth, he didn't have a whole lot of experience dealing with women. There had been a few in his life, but even when sex was involved he'd taken pains to keep it chummy. That way, when the sensual fire went out, they could part friends.

He'd held back because in the back of his mind, there had always been the fearful notion that he might get swept up in a moment of bliss and propose to the wrong woman. As a morbid spectator to Riley's disastrous union, he'd avoided the issue of marriage like a green colt avoided the saddle.

Marriage? Was that even a consideration here? Maybe so, but he'd be damned if he knew what to do about it right now. He was going to miss that plane. Maybe some time apart was what they needed. When he was with Noelle, he had a hard time remaining rational.

When Brody didn't respond, Noelle assumed he agreed with her. "Brody?"

"I don't want to mess this up," he said desperately. "We have something special."

"I don't deny that." But how special could it be when he hadn't so much as hinted at a future for them? It was time she realized that being the best damn quarter horse trainer in the country came first in his life. She and the boys would always run a pale second.

She'd lived like that before and it had exacted an emotional toll that she couldn't bear again. "The risks are too great, Brody. I guess we're what you'd call a long shot."

"Okay," he said in exasperation. "You're scared. Well, so am I. But I've never let fear stop me and I'll bet you haven't, either."

"I don't know."

"Don't shut me out, Noelle. I'll call you from Ruidoso and we'll talk about this."

"Do what you want to do, Brody. Now you'd better get on that plane." And with that Noelle hung up. She sat and stared at the phone for a long time, wondering if she'd done the right thing.

She'd known this day would come and that she'd have to make a decision. But damned if she didn't feel ill-equipped to make it. Brody's work and life-style weren't conducive to the family life she wanted so badly. He worked long days, seven days a week, and by his own admission he hadn't had a vacation in ten years. She wanted someone she could count on, someone who needed her. Brody didn't need anyone.

Before she could feel too sorry for herself, Darcy stopped by her desk. "What's up? You look like your dog just died."

"Nothing so simple." She explained what had happened, as well as her doubts."

"Be careful, friend," Darcy warned. "Don't compare Brody to Steve."

"I'm not."

"I think you are. Give Brody time to come to terms with his feelings. Give him time to learn to love you."

"What do you mean?"

"In some ways I know him better than you do. When Riley drinks, he likes to talk. And what he talks about is Brody. Brody works because it's all he knows. And right now Riley is such a mess that Brody has to do the work of two men."

"Tell me about it, Darcy."

"I can't, hon," Darcy said with a gentle pat on Noelle's shoulder. "It wouldn't be fair. He'll tell you when he's ready. Give him time. When he realizes what a good thing he has in you, he'll come around."

"Do you think so?"

"Time, Noelle. Be patient. Brody won't hurt you."

"Easy for you to say."

"Easy for me to know."

Brody called late that night. "I hope I didn't wake you, but I just got back to the motel."

Noelle sat up in bed and propped a pillow behind her. "How's the horse?"

"We saved him, but he's out of the Futurity trials and he'll wind up missing the rest of his two-year-old races."

"I'm sorry."

"Hey, these things happen. Racehorses are basically dumb critters and so many things can go wrong that it boggles the mind. We have several other strong horses in training and I feel one of them will take home the purse on Labor Day.''

"I'm glad to hear that. I know how important it is to you."

Her words echoed the twins' and he flinched. "I'm lonely as hell,'' he admitted.

"I'm perversely glad to hear that.''

"I hope that means you haven't given up on me.'' It was easier to express his insecurities with miles of telephone cable stretched between them.

"I don't want to give up, Brody, but sometimes I'm afraid to keep going.'' She couldn't bear the pain of losing him any more than she could bear the pain of loving him.

"Hang in there, kid. It'll get better. I'm going to talk to Riley when I get back and see if I can get him straightened out. If he'll take over some of the load, I'll have more time.''

Noelle wondered if she should mention what Darcy had told her about Riley's drinking. Maybe she was right about the family turning a blind eye. "Darcy's worried about Riley,'' she said to open the subject.

"Yeah, I know. Darcy's a sweet kid, I'm sorry she's mixed up in this. I've gotten him out of one scrape after another since we were kids, but this time I don't know how to help him.''

"Maybe it's time Riley helped himself,'' she suggested gently. "He's not a little boy anymore and you may have to let him grow up and take care of himself.''

"Are you saying he'll resent my help?''

"Maybe. Wouldn't you resent someone trying to run your life?''

"Sure, but...'' Brody's voice trailed off. "You may be right. Being big brother to Riley is getting to be a full-time job. But I'd hate to think of him getting thrown in the drunk tank."

"It could prove to be the catalyst he needs to get professional help. There are some good clinics with dependency programs."

"All the programs in the world won't help Riley unless he's willing to be helped. I'll try to talk some sense into him. In the meantime, there's something I want to ask you."

"What's that?"

"Ruby and Dub have been after me to bring you and the boys out to their place for a visit when I get back to town."

"We'd love to go," Noelle said, not giving herself a chance to think about it. By meeting his foster family, she might find the key to understanding him. "When do you think you'll be back?"

"I'm not sure but, it can't be soon enough to suit me."

Brody continued to call her every night at bedtime and he shared his work with her, if not his feelings. She told him how much the twins missed him and their previous rift was forgotten—or ignored. Noelle knew that nothing had been resolved, but she pretended not to care. Maybe life with Brody wasn't in the cards. But life without him was too terrible to consider.

Although it was far from boring, twelve days of courting over the wire was frustrating. Brody needed to see Noelle, to hold her. So, the night before he planned to come back he called earlier than usual.

"Hello?" a small voice answered tentatively.

"Hello." Brody grinned. "Is this Dusty or Danny or Ralph?"

"Danny."

"This is Brody, how're you doing, buddy?"

"Fine, but me and Dusty's not s'posed to answer the phone or the door."

"Where's your momma? Is everything all right?"

"I think so," he replied, his voice slightly muffled by a rustling noise.

"What's going on there?" The potential for mischief was unlimited.

There was an indignant squeal in the background and Dusty's voice came on the line. "Hi, Brody, it's me, Dusty."

"What happened to Danny?"

"Aww, he's mad 'cause it's my turn to talk."

"Where's your momma?"

"She's takin' a shower."

Understanding dawned. "You and Danny aren't supposed to answer the phone when she's in there, are you?"

"Nah, but it was only you."

"You didn't know that before you answered," he pointed out.

"I didn't answer, Danny did."

"Where were you?"

"I had to let the paper boy in. It's time to collect," he explained importantly.

"You let him in the house?" Brody exclaimed.

"Naw, he said he'd come back later."

"Dusty, will you do something for me?"

"Sure, Brody."

"Do you know how to lock the door?"

"Aw, heck, I'm four." His tone implied that only a total dolt would ask a four-year-old if he knew how to lock the door.

"That's what I want you to do. Go lock the front door right now. Okay?"

"Okay," he replied in an if-that's-what-you-want tone.

Click. The line was filled with dead air.

"Damn!" Brody hung up, counted to ten, then dialed again.

"Hello."

"Danny?"

"Yeah?"

"Where's Dusty?"

"He went to lock the door like you said."

"Is your mother still in the shower?"

"Uh-huh."

"Then why did you answer the phone? Never mind, just go tell her I want to talk to her. Can you do that?"

"Sure, Brody. 'Bye."

"No, no, don't hang up!" he yelled too late.

Brody forced himself to wait a full five minutes before dialing.

"Don't ever do that again," he ordered the moment Noelle answered the phone.

"Hello to you, too. Don't do what again?"

"Do you realize the twins answered the phone and the door while you were in the shower?"

"They told me."

"You're pretty blasé. What if it'd been some psycho at the door or some pervert on the phone?"

"I could give up taking showers, Brody, but somehow I don't think you'd like me as much," she teased.

"I'm sorry, but you can't imagine how I felt when Dusty told me he had let the paper boy in."

"The paper boy is eleven years old and lives down the block. The pervert on the telephone was you. How was your day?"

"Great. Five of my horses qualified for the time trials."

"Congratulations. That's pretty good isn't it?"

"Yeah, it's pretty good." Brody chuckled at the understatement. "I can see now that you still have a lot to learn about the horse training business. And I think it'll be fun teaching you."

"I've been doing some studying on my own, but when's the first lesson?"

"How's tomorrow night? I can get away for a few days and I need to check on things out at Cimarron." What he needed to check on was Riley. Billy had called to tell Brody that he hadn't seen him for two days.

"Will you be here in time for dinner?"

"Yes, but Ruby's been driving me crazy. Glory's home for a short visit and they all want to meet you. If you're willing, we can go out there tomorrow night and get it over with."

"Get it over with? You make it sound like you're going for dental surgery."

"It's not that. It's just that I've never introduced the family to anyone I was seeing and I'm afraid they'll jump to all kinds of wrong conclusions. But I'm willing to risk it if you are."

"I don't know. I'd hate for your family to think there was anything 'serious' going on." Noelle cursed the pouty note she detected in her voice.

"I'll handle them. I'll pick you up around six and then on Sunday we can take the boys to Frontier City. Do you think they'd like that?"

"Do I think two kids with a cowboy fixation would like spending the day at a Western theme park? Gee, I don't know."

Brody laughed at his own silly question. "Later we'll go out to Cimarron. It's high time I showed you around."

Noelle couldn't agree more.

Chapter Ten

Noelle went over the basic rules of good behavior with Dusty and Danny while they were waiting for Brody to arrive. Her anxiety about the trip to Phoenix Farms to meet the Roberts soon communicated itself to the twins. Then she had to worry, not only about making a good impression, but about her sons' behavior.

What if Brody's family didn't approve of her? Or worse, what if they did and attached too much significance to the visit? She hadn't forgotten Brody's reluctant invitation.

She needn't have worried. Dub and Ruby met them at the door of the rambling ranch house and from the very first moment the couple's warmth and friendliness made Noelle feel right at home.

Dub's ready grin and merry ways put her in mind of an overgrown leprechaun. He treated Dusty and Danny like long-lost grandchildren and they responded to his teasing and roughhousing with the unabashed joy children find in making a new friend.

Ruby Roberts, who in her own words was as wide as she was tall, had springy gray curls and a sun-wrinkled face. When Noelle expressed concern over the boys' romping, Ruby told her not to worry about a thing, proclaiming the house had been without children's laughter way too long.

Glory Roberts, whose wide eyes were the same shade of golden brown as her hair, was the darling of the clan. Her parents, rightfully proud of the recently graduated equine vet, embarrassed her by extolling her many accomplishments.

Glory was home for a short visit before leaving for the University of California on a research grant. In a year she'd be coming home to begin her practice right here at Phoenix Farms.

Dub and Ruby weren't the only ones proud of Glory. Dub's station manager, Ross Forbes, who seemed ill at ease in the family setting, displayed a quiet interest in everything she had to say.

While Dub and Ruby treated Ross more like a son than an employee, it was clear to Noelle that Glory's feelings for the broodingly handsome cowboy were far from sisterly. The young woman made no secret of her infatuation, but he carefully pretended not to notice.

"It's great to be home," Glory told Brody. "I've missed everyone so much." She spoke to the family, but her eyes were on Ross.

Ross obviously felt the scrutiny because he looked up and remarked, "The place hasn't been the same without you, brat."

"Kind of boring and lonely, huh?"

He shrugged dismissively. "Peaceful's more like it."

Glory sighed melodramatically and everyone at the dining table laughed.

Riley was conspicuously absent, but Noelle knew better than to ask questions. Brody had already told her that he'd been out of touch with the family for a few days. He tried to act unconcerned, but she could sense an underlying anxiety, not only in Brody, but in Dub and Ruby, as well. Maybe Riley wasn't just absent. Maybe he was missing.

By the time the roast beef and potatoes had been consumed, Noelle had forgotten why she'd ever worried about coming. Brody's family was such a loving, giving, group that she couldn't understand why it was so hard for him to open up. Perhaps someday he'd tell her.

"Enjoying yourself?" Brody asked her as they cleared the table.

"Very much. Thanks for inviting us."

Ruby took the empty plates from Brody. "You young people run along and find something to do while Pap and I clean up."

At Noelle's protest Dub added, "Me and Ruby always do KP together. It's a habit we got into when we started collecting all these kids. It was our time to discuss and cuss our personal business, 'cause it was the only time we could be sure none of 'em would come bustin' in on us."

Ruby elbowed him good-naturedly. "The children weren't so bad. As I recollect we had plenty of privacy."

"Yeah," he agreed with an ornery grin. "But we never did much talking in the bedroom, Ma."

Ruby's sun-darkened face flushed red and she slapped him playfully on the arm. "Hush, you old coot. You're just awful."

Before she could dance away with her armload of dishes, Dub patted her ample backside. "That's why you married me in the first place, wasn't it?"

Laughing, Brody led the others outside to the big wraparound porch with its two porch swings and pots of geraniums. The days were growing shorter now as summer slumped toward fall and the deep shadows of evening were a welcome respite from the heat. Insects hummed in the lilac bushes and somewhere a dog barked.

Brody sat down with Noelle on one of the swings, the twins between them. He hadn't had a moment alone with her and he ached for more than the brief kiss of greeting they'd shared earlier. He put his arm across the back of the swing and stroked her shoulder.

Glory sat in the opposite swing and patted the cushion beside her. "Sit here, Ross. There's plenty of room."

"This is fine," he drawled as he elevated one booted foot on the bottom of the porch rail and folded his arms across his knee. "Heard your good news about the time trials, Brody. Congratulations, man."

"Thanks. I knew I had some prime racing stock this year, but it's a great feeling when they prove you right."

"With the All-American only a week away, I'm surprised you aren't in Ruidoso with your nose to the grindstone." Ross seemed well acquainted with Brody's work habits.

Brody and Glory exchanged a nervous glance and Noelle knew they were thinking of Riley. "Something came up. I'll be heading back Monday."

"How's Overnight Sensation doing? Having any more trouble with that old injury of his?"

"Not a bit, he's in fine form. He told me he was going to win the All-American this year and I believe him."

"Do horses really talk?" Dusty asked incredulously.

"Like *Mister Ed* on TV?" Danny, who was a big fan of ancient reruns, wanted to know.

Glory laughed. "They only talk to Brody, boys. No one else can hear them."

"Horses don't talk with their mouths," Brody explained. "But when you spend as much time with them as I do, you learn to listen to their actions."

"I've seen Brody in action," Ross put in. "He's so tuned in to his horses, that he instinctively knows when to push them and when to let up. It's amazing. He gets so attached to his animals that he treats 'em like family."

"He keeps one old nag in his pasture that can't do anything but eat," Glory teased.

"Guilty," Brody admitted sheepishly. "Pass 'Em's a pure pet."

"Can we ride him?"

"Pass 'Em's a girl and sure you can ride her sometime."

"Yippee," the twins chorused.

Brody smiled at Noelle over the boys' blond heads and longed for a few minutes alone with her. Maybe when Dusty and Danny went away to college they could do some serious lovemaking, he thought.

Ross must have heard Brody's sigh because he said suddenly, "How would you boys like to see some brand-new baby horses?"

"Good idea, Ross, I'll come too." Glory was quick to invite herself along. "No visit to a breeding station is complete without seeing a foal or two."

"Can we, Momma, can we?"

"If you'll agree to obey Ross and Glory." Noelle had figured out what was going on and thanked Brody's sister with a knowing smile.

After they departed, the boys skipping and hopping between the adults, Brody slid across the porch swing until he was as close to Noelle as he could get. He gathered her into his arms and whispered, ''I thought they'd never get the hint.''

''Brody.'' Noelle's protest wasn't really meant or taken as one. ''The place is crawling with people. Someone might see us.''

''Let 'em.'' His mouth opened boldly over hers and his hand skimmed possessively over her back, down her hip and around her waist. He tugged her close and molded her soft curves to his muscular chest.

Noelle recognized the intensity of his desire, it flamed hot with urgency. Wrapping her arms around his neck, she deepened the kiss. She reveled in the powerful persuasion of his tongue as it penetrated her lips and delved into her mouth in an exciting rhythm.

Brody groaned as Noelle pressed against him. Desire for her sang through his body and never before had he felt such unadulterated need. He released her lips and placed hot little kisses on her eyes, her jaw, her chin. Then he nuzzled her neck with gentle love bites.

''If we keep this up, I can't be held responsible for what happens,'' he told her, his breath coming in ragged gasps.

''Me, either.''

He held her face in his hands. ''Someday, I won't be able to stop.''

Noelle outlined his lips with her fingertip and ached with the love she felt for him. ''I know.''

''I wish you were this agreeable about everything,'' he growled. He pulled her to her feet. ''Come on, let's go check on the boys before this gets too hot to handle.''

She smiled up at him, slightly dazed by her response. "The mood you've just put me in, I'd follow you anywhere."

He grasped her hips and wiggled against her. "You mean if I were to suggest someplace more intimate than a porch swing right now, you'd be receptive?"

"Kiss me like that again and I'd be receptive in the middle of Lazy E Arena," she teased. "Now come on, we'd better find the others. There's safety in numbers, you know."

They caught up with Ross, Glory and the twins in one of the foaling barns. Danny and Dusty ran to them, as quiet as they could be, out of deference to the location.

"Guess what?" Danny gushed.

"You got to see a baby horse, right?" Noelle was grateful for the boys' happiness. Brody's family had given them something very special today—unconditional acceptance.

"*Two* babies. Twins," Dusty exclaimed.

"Like us," his brother supplied in case she hadn't figured that out.

The boys led Brody and Noelle to the stall where the spindly legged foals wobbled and nudged each other as they vied for their dinner. Their big-eyed mother stood patiently, occasionally stamping a hoof when they pulled on the teats too hard.

Ross excused himself, claiming he had to drive over to a neighboring ranch to pick up a piece of equipment.

"It was nice meeting you," Noelle told him. "Thanks for showing the boys around."

"No problem, ma'am," he said respectfully. "They're fine boys." He tipped his hat. "Maybe I'll see you around here again sometime."

"You can bet on that," Brody told him.

"Hey, Ross?" Glory's tone was a study of nonchalance. "Since you're going over to Harvey's..."

"No," he said, rather too quickly. "You can't go."

"Why not? I heard Larry Dale was home for a visit. I'd like to see him again."

"Suit yourself, brat." A muscle twitched in Ross's lean jaw as he spun on his heel and stalked out of the barn.

"You shouldn't do that, Glory," Brody chastised.

"Do what?" she asked innocently.

"You don't care a thing for Larry Dale but you've been dangling him in front of Ross since you were a kid."

"Yeah, I know." She grinned. "It still works, too. Puffs him up like a green bronc on a cold morning."

"Why can't you leave the poor guy alone?" her brother asked.

"That's his problem," she said with a toss of her long hair. "The old cuss has been alone too long. I see you've mellowed out considerably since you met Noelle. It's amazing what a good woman can do for a man." She grinned at Noelle and winked before hurrying after Ross.

Brody called after her. "Ross is right, Sis, you are a brat."

They turned their attention back to the boys who were still oohing and aahing over the nursing foals.

"How old are they, Brody?" Danny asked.

He looked them over with a practiced eye. "I'd guess about a week."

"Gosh," Dusty marveled. "They can walk and everything. Could we walk when we was a week old, Momma?"

"No." She smiled at the wonder nature could inspire in the very young. "You were much smaller than these babies."

"We could eat as good as they can though, couldn't we?" Danny asked.

Noelle's smile faded into an embarrassed flush when she recalled the effort breast-feeding twins had been. She looked up and saw Brody choking on his laughter.

"Just about," she managed before dissolving into nervous giggles.

"What's so funny?" Danny asked his brother.

Dusty shrugged eloquently. "Heck if I know. Some grown-up stuff prob'ly."

Noelle had never taken the twins to the wild and wooly amusement park known as Frontier City. As so often happened with locals, she had overlooked an attraction that pulled in tourists from all over the state. She hadn't thought the boys were old enough to enjoy it, but they soon proved her wrong. Since meeting Brody they were deeply interested in all things having to do with cowboys.

After only a few minutes it became clear that Brody was having as much fun as the children. He accompanied them on all the big rides and stood on the sidelines and waved while they rode the ones designed for the junior set.

"You must have loved this place when you were a kid," Noelle observed.

Brody's smile dissolved. "By the time Riley and I went to live with Ruby and Dub we thought we were too old for it. We were careful never to ask them for any special favors."

Noelle hoped this was the opening she had been waiting for. "Why? They certainly seem generous enough."

"Oh, they'd give you the shirt off their backs," he concurred. "But we were afraid that if we asked for anything they wouldn't want us anymore. Living in foster homes taught us that much."

"Tell me about it, Brody," she urged softly.

He hesitated a moment, and then when he looked into her eyes and saw genuine caring and concern there, a dam started breaking. A dam that he'd built and cemented over long, painful years.

"I don't remember much about my mother except that she was sick most of the time. We lived in a little tar-paper shack in Talihina near the Ouachita Mountains. Mother died when Riley was two. Our father wasn't much for child rearing, so I mostly took care of us."

"But you were just a baby yourself," Noelle exclaimed, shocked by the thought that a parent could be so insensitive.

"I was nearly six. I didn't mind taking care of Riley, he was a sweet kid. He was always laughing and happy to see me, he looked up to me. Joe Sawyer held that those who didn't work didn't eat and I was afraid he might leave us, so I worked twice as hard. He wasn't much of a father, but he was all we had."

"But wasn't there some kind of child protection service? Or welfare?"

"We were pretty far back in the sticks, remember. Not many social workers tramped those hills looking for poor, mistreated children."

"Didn't you have any relatives?"

"None that I knew of. Our mother claimed some people in Kentucky, but I never knew who they were."

"So, you became Riley's protector?" Noelle began to understand things a bit better.

"I tried to be. More often than not, I ended up taking the brunt of our father's wrath."

"Oh, Brody, you don't mean he abused you?" She felt her heart constrict with the enormity of what he was telling her. She couldn't imagine anyone hurting a child, much less the child's own parent.

"It wasn't that bad. Joe didn't hang around much. Mostly, he left us to ourselves which was fine with us. Things got a little tricky when I started to go to school."

"You mean you had to leave Riley alone?"

"No, he was too little so I took him to school on the bus with me. There was a park nearby and in warm weather he played there until I got out. Then it turned cold, and I hid him in the janitor's closet. Mr. Walker was a kind black man who came in to clean after school hours. One day he caught us as we were leaving the supply closet."

"What happened?"

"I guess he felt sorry for us. He started meeting me at the bus in the morning. He'd take Riley to spend the day with his wife while he worked in a gas station. Then she'd walk Riley to the bus stop in the afternoon and we'd ride home."

"Oh, Brody." No wonder there was such a strong bond between the brothers. They'd had to depend on each other to survive. "Didn't anyone at the school, a teacher or the bus driver, ever figure out what was going on?"

"If they did, they never said anything. Most of the kids in the school were poor, we weren't so different. When I was nine, Joe got a wild idea and moved us here to Oklahoma City."

"Did things improve?"

"Depends on how you look at it." Brody stared at the kiddie ride, watching the tiny helicopters filled with shrieking children and remembered. His eyes turned cold.

"Joe left us with a woman he'd taken up with, said he was going to look for work. Promised he'd be back. But days turned into weeks and after a few of those, with no word from Joe, his lady friend turned us over to the welfare department. For the next year or so we played musical foster homes."

"Is that where Dub and Ruby came in?"

He shook his head. "No, but lucky for us that's where we finally ended up. They weren't like the other places, they didn't take in children for the money the state paid them. They just liked kids. To a couple of rag-tails like me and Riley, they seemed like millionaires. That big house and the farm was paradise."

Noelle could only imagine how Brody and Riley must have basked in the security of their new home. How the country sunshine and farm work had made them strong. "They seem like wonderful parents. I take it Glory is their natural child."

"Yeah. I think they were in their late forties and had given up hope of ever having children when she came along. She was just a little tyke when we went to live with them and she won us over right off. But it took us a while to believe Dub and Ruby really wanted us."

"And you never heard from your father?" Noelle had read of child abandonment, but the reality was so much more terrible.

"We weren't that lucky. After about three years, Joe finally showed up and the welfare worker made us see him. He claimed he'd been looking for us and was ready to take us home. Wherever that was."

"What did you do?"

"Dub and Ruby asked us if we wanted to go with him and of course we didn't. We had a place with them and it was a good place. Neither of us wanted to leave with a man who was nothing more than a stranger."

"In most custody situations that I've heard of, the courts try to reunite the children with their natural parents."

"They tried, but Dub and Ruby fought for us. They were granted permanent custody when old Joe decided to give up his parental rights."

"Decided?"

"I found out years later that Dub had paid him off. I'll be grateful to him for the rest of my life for that. If it weren't for Dub and Ruby, Riley and I wouldn't have a thing. Not knowledge, not skills, not self-respect."

"And you haven't seen your father since?"

"He looked us up in Ruidoso a few years ago. He had a job at the track mucking out stables and when he heard about us he stopped by to say hello. Riley's always been a sucker for a sob story and wanted to take the old man home with us and take care of him."

"How did you feel about that?"

"At first I was madder than hell. Maybe Riley didn't remember what that man had done to us, but I sure did. I went to see Joe myself and offered him money to stay away from us. It had worked once, so I figured it might work again. He broke down and cried."

"That must have been traumatic."

"I wasn't mad anymore," he admitted quietly. "Joe said he'd done that once, he wouldn't do it again. He promised he'd never bother us again. So far, that's the only promise he ever kept."

Noelle now understood so many things. Why Brody pushed himself so hard to succeed. Why he used cynicism to mask his tender heart. Now she knew why he was so protective of Riley. It wasn't commitment he was afraid of, it was breaking promises. She reached out to him and touched his arm, trying to communicate some of the understanding she felt.

"It's hard for me to accept that a man could, in effect, sell his children. But I guess what Steve did isn't so very different," she said softly.

"Maybe everything will work out for the best," he said. "It did for us. Selling us out was the only good thing Joe ever did. At least we grew up with a feeling of worth. Dub and Ruby gave us that."

"I'm glad you told me, Brody." She smiled and slipped her hand in his. "The ride's over. Let's go get the dynamic duo."

"Did you see us flyin' by?" Dusty called as he ran toward them.

"We were going so fast, everything was blurry," Danny exclaimed.

"That looked like thirsty work to me," Brody drawled in his cowboy voice. "Whaddya say we mosey on down to the saloon and get ourselves a frosty mug of root beer?"

"Good idea," Noelle agreed. "I heard there might be a gunfight soon."

The boys gulped down their root beers in the Pink Garter Saloon and Soda Fountain and watched wide-eyed as a full-blown ruckus developed right before their eyes.

The deputy rushed into the saloon to inform the sheriff that the bank had been robbed and the outlaws were getting away. The lawman shoved a Miss Kitty lookalike off his lap and raced out the door.

The gunfight staged outdoors on Main Street was straight out of the Western movies. Dusty and Danny had to be held up in Brody's strong arms so as not to miss a single thing. They clapped their hands over their ears every time a blank cartridge exploded.

Just when it seemed the good guys had prevailed and law and order was once more restored, a bandit—hidden in a nearby tree—fired at the sheriff who collapsed from a mock wound in the leg.

But being a tough frontier peacekeeper, the sheriff rolled to his back and shot the outlaw right out of the tree.

The dust cleared and the audience applauded. Good guys and bad guys alike stood and took their bows, dusting off their vintage clothing with their hats. They mingled with the crowd and talked to the children, making sure that even the youngest ones understood that it had all been part of the entertainment.

It was early evening by the time they talked the boys into leaving. Brody led them into a souvenir shop and, despite Noelle's objections about violence, bought the boys plastic holsters and toy guns.

"The guys know what's real and what's pretend, don't you fellas?"

Dusty and Danny nodded solemnly, but for good measure Brody lectured them about gun safety all the way home. They'd lingered too long at the park and agreed to postpone the trip to Cimarron until the next day, Sunday. Brody was leaving for New Mexico on Monday to get ready for the All-American Futurity.

After they tucked the tired children into bed, Noelle asked if he'd like a cup of coffee.

"If I stay, we both know it wouldn't be for coffee. And something tells me this isn't the time or the place."

"You're very astute, cowboy."

Wrapping an arm around her shoulders he guided her toward the front door. "So, I'll settle for a raincheck and an extremely passionate good-night kiss."

Noelle twined her arms around his neck and stood on tiptoe. "That I can arrange."

He traced her bottom lip with his tongue before placing his mouth over hers, pulling her up into his arms until her toes dangled a few inches from the floor. Her breasts flattened against his wildly hammering heart as he held her in a powerful embrace. When he relaxed his hold she slid down his body, limp with the desire he provoked.

"We have to stop meeting like this," she gasped.

He allowed his lips to brush over hers before tearing them away. Still holding her loosely Brody said, "I'd better go, or else."

"Or else what?"

"Or else the boys wake up in the morning and find me in their mother's bed. You don't want that do you?"

Her hands slid from his neck, down his arms. She smiled. "Yes, and no."

"That's what I thought." He squeezed her to him. "I'll pick you up at eight in the morning."

"You don't have to make it that early," she protested. "I know you have a lot of work to do."

"Hey, lady. I'm no layabout. I'll have put in several hours by then. Besides, I want to spend as much time as possible with you and the boys before I leave."

His words thrilled her. Not only that he wanted to be with them, but that he had finally admitted it out loud. Maybe their talk this afternoon had helped him as much as it had helped her. At least it was a step in the right direction.

"Okay, but give me directions and we'll come to you. It'll save you an extra trip into town."

He complied. "Come for breakfast, I'll rustle up something."

"You're a good man, Brody Sawyer. You'll make some woman a good husband one of these days," she teased.

He knew she was joking, but he was completely serious when he finally answered, "Maybe I will, at that."

He buried his face in her hair, savoring the feel of her softness as she melted against the hard contours of his body. Her urgent response was nearly his undoing. He needed and wanted her with an intensity that unnerved him.

But somehow, after unburdening himself to her this afternoon, it didn't scare him as much as it once had. Tomorrow would be special. Tomorrow he'd talk to her, share his feelings. He'd do and say all the right things to tighten the bond that had formed between them despite their reservations and fears.

Tomorrow, he'd make a promise that he'd keep for the rest of his life.

Chapter Eleven

Noelle drove under the arched sign of Cimarron Racing Stables at nine the next morning. The day promised to be hot and sunny, typical of end-of-August weather. In the back seat Dusty and Danny squirmed and wiggled as much as their safety restraints allowed, trying to see everything at once.

Behind white pole fencing on either side of the drive, horses grazed. The beautiful animals raised their sleek heads curiously as the visitors drove past.

Massed spirea bordered the road. Noelle's grandmother had called them "popcorn" bushes because in the spring they exploded with clusters of showy, snowy flowers.

Beyond the house she saw a number of weathered red barns and outbuildings gleaming with white trim and corrals constructed of the same white poles as the fence.

In the far fields newly-baled hay dried in the sun. Everywhere Noelle looked there was a sense of care and order. Following Brody's instructions she stopped the car in front of a sprawling ranch house built of rock and weather-silvered cedar.

The architect had carefully preserved the on-site timber and the house nestled among the tall sycamores and oaks like a work of nature. The trees were motionless in the still morning air, as if lost in listening to the birds twittering in their branches.

Underground sprinklers shot water over the bermuda grass lawn with a steady, *ka-chook, ka-chook, ka-chook,* and tiny rainbows shimmered in the spray. Colorful New Guinea impatiens brightened the shady corners of the yard, and dwarf marigolds spilled out of the flower borders. Someone, and Noelle was sure it wasn't Brody, spent a lot of time doing yard work.

As she hustled the boys out of the car, they spotted a clutch of long-eared beagle puppies stumbling over one another in their race around the corner of the house.

The boys ran after them and when Noelle followed, she found Brody standing on a redwood deck in back. Waving, he pushed away from the railing and strode toward her, puppies yipping at his heels. He was wearing snug jeans and a chambray shirt open at the throat. He was bare-headed for a change and the sun danced on his dark brown hair.

Passing the boys, who by this time were tumbling on the ground with the puppies, he stooped to ruffle their hair. He caught Noelle's gaze and held it as he approached, a big smile of welcome on his face. She felt herself start to glow and vibrate in anticipation of his kiss and was filled with renewed conviction.

She loved him. She couldn't help it.

"You made it," he said after the sweet, lingering kiss she'd hoped for. "Did you have any trouble finding the place?"

"None. You give good directions." Standing with his arm around her shoulder, she drank in the serenity of her surroundings. Cimarron was only a few miles from the urban sprawl of Oklahoma City, but it could have been a hundred. There were no exhaust fumes to spoil the heavy verdancy of the air, no city sounds to break the country quiet.

"It's beautiful here," she told him. "This is exactly how I pictured you living."

Brody recalled the tar-paper shack of his childhood and laughed. "Yeah, me, too. Come on, I'll show you around inside while the boys play with the dogs."

Noelle made them promise to stay on the deck before she followed Brody through the back door and into the house. They stepped into a kitchen with white counter-tops and oak cabinets. Noelle appreciatively sniffed the aroma of fresh coffee. A slim, middle-aged Native American woman looked up from a frying pan of siz-zling bacon. Brody introduced her as Wanda Sixkiller.

"Her husband Billy is a great hand with horses," he teased. "But the only reason I keep him around is for Wanda's cooking. Wait'll you taste her blueberry waf-fles."

Wanda smiled shyly as Brody and Noelle passed through the kitchen on the way to the living room. The airy room had many windows, high ceilings and an en-tire wall made of the same gray rock as the outside. A beautiful Navaho rug covered the wood floor in front of the hearth on which perched a whimsical clay coyote, that was posed as if to howl at the moon.

The room's color scheme of blue, cream and wine was borrowed from the Indian rug and woven pillows in muted shades were scattered over the leather sofas. Earthenware pottery and baskets filled with dried flowers continued the Southwestern motif and Noelle recognized some of the paintings by local North American artists.

"What do you think?" Brody asked, anxious for her to approve of his home.

"It's magnificent. I don't know how you can bear to be away so much. If I had a house like this, I'd never want to leave it," she enthused.

That's what he was counting on. "Before I met you, I never paid much attention to things around the house. I was more interested in the barns and equipment. Then, all of a sudden this place seemed depressing and empty. I gave Wanda my credit cards and sent her shopping. She seemed to know exactly what I wanted."

"Really? I assumed it had been done by a professional decorator." Noelle glanced around and saw Wanda, clearly embarrassed by the honest praise, standing in the doorway.

"Thank you, ma'am," she said. "But I didn't do so much. Brody and I went through some magazines until he found what he liked. All I did was tote it home."

"Don't let her fool you, Noelle. Wanda has a great sense of style."

The woman beamed. "Breakfast is ready, folks. I called in the boys and they're washing up in the kitchen."

The waffles were every bit as good as promised, but they all ate quickly so they could see the rest of Cimarron. Brody pointed out the house where Billy and Wanda lived and a group of trailer homes for the other married employees. A bunkhouse next to the barn housed the single men.

"It must be handy to have the help live at the ranch," Noelle remarked.

"With the crazy hours ranch work demands, it's the best arrangement. This way, the men can go home during the off-hours and be with their families."

Noelle spotted another big house visible through a stand of trees. "Who lives there?"

"That's Riley's place."

"Is he home yet?" she asked, her concern evident. She knew Darcy hadn't heard from him for several days and wondered if he'd been in touch with Brody.

"Not yet. I don't know where he is. It's not like him to just take off, though. I'm afraid something might have happened."

"Are you going to call the police?" she asked.

"And tell them what? That my brother got drunk and forgot to phone home? I don't think so." He quickly dropped the painful subject.

They went on to the main barn where the horses were kept. "It's practically empty now," he explained. "We have only thirty or so head. Most of them are at Ruidoso Downs. Because it's Sunday and between feeding times, I'm afraid there isn't much activity going on around here today."

Inside the barn were clean, roomy stalls for each horse. The building was not nearly as *fragrant* as Noelle had expected a barn to be and she could only wonder at the amount of work required to keep things so neat. When they drew near the first stall, the animal inside snuffled a greeting and stuck its head over the top of the gate.

"This is Velvet," Brody told the boys. He picked them up so they could stroke the mare's long neck.

"She kissed me!" Dusty exclaimed when the mare nosed his hand.

"She's hoping you brought her a bite of carrot." He set the boys down and directed them to a basket full of carrots in the corner. They were back in an instant for Brody to demonstrate proper carrot-feeding technique.

He glanced up and noticed Noelle watching him. "What are you thinking?"

Since it wouldn't do to tell him that she thought he'd make a wonderful father, she improvised. "I was thinking Velvet is a strange name for a racehorse."

"Her real name is Take A Fast Plane. When we get a colt in here we can't always get their papers the same day. Or sometimes, they don't have a name yet. We try to pick out one that fits. We called her Velvet because her coat looks like black velvet. That's one of the nicer nicknames."

He led her to the next stall. "For instance, this one makes a puddle every time you get behind her so we call her..."

"Let me guess. Puddles?"

"You've been doing your homework," he commended her with a crooked grin.

"Do any of these belong to you?"

"Riley and I have a few mares stabled at Dub's, but the rest of our stock is turned out to pasture. Some of them are too old to race and some never had the heart for it in the first place. But I can't bring myself to get rid of them, so we just give them a home."

"You like to talk tough, Sawyer," she accused. "But you're just an old softy."

"Maybe so. Will Rogers said he never met a man he didn't like. That's how I feel about horses."

He led them outside to the barn where the yearlings were broken. It was round, with no corners for the young horses to run into and hurt themselves or their riders. Brody pointed out the exercise walkers and the twins were quick to observe that the machines looked like merry-go-rounds for horses.

About that time two little boys, a bit older than Dusty and Danny, came out of one of the trailers. The oldest one cupped his hands around his mouth and called, "Hey, Brody, can them boys come and play with us on the swings?"

"Can we, Momma?" they asked.

"That's Tommy and Terry," Brody told Noelle. "Their father has worked here for a couple of years now. They're pretty safe company."

The twins scampered off just as a tall Native American man walked up. Brody introduced Noelle to his top hand, Billy Sixkiller. His coppery face was weather beaten, his dark eyes kind. He wore a Western shirt, blue jeans and boots. Under his straight-brimmed hat, Billy's long gray hair was tied at his nape with a strip of leather.

Billy's black eyes twinkled with mischief. "Nice to meet ya, Miz Chandler. Now I know why this boy's been spendin' so much time on airplanes lately. Wanda said you were pretty and I'm inclined to agree with her."

Noelle smiled. "Thank you."

"I couldn't believe it when she told me about the little shavers, though. I never knowed the boy here to take much to young'uns before. He never even allowed Riley's kids inside his door."

"Don't pay any attention to him, Noelle," Brody told her. "Dusty and Danny are nothing like those two."

"Maybe you haven't spent enough time with them, after all," she countered.

Billy went right on. "I've been with this boy ever since he started the place. He's always been a fair boss, but since he met you, he's been downright pleasant."

Brody looked embarrassed and Noelle looked pleased. He took her arm. "Come on, I want to show you my pride and joy."

He led her to a six furlong regulation racetrack on which he trained horses and jockeys. Both sides of the track were lined with small bushes that would one day grow into a substantial hedge.

"It took every hand on the place a whole weekend to plant those bushes," Brody told her. "I lost count, but I think there's over four thousand of the little devils."

"Wouldn't it have been easier to put up a fence?" she asked.

"Easier, yes. Safer, no. If an unpredictable colt ducks into a fence, the rider could be crippled. If he falls into the hedge he just gets scratched up a little."

They reached one of the pasture fences and Brody propped his booted foot on the bottom rail and whistled. An aged dappled horse trotted over the rise and when it saw Brody, galloped the rest of the way. The horse nuzzled his shirt pocket and whinnied. Brody chuckled and produced a sugar cube.

"This is the infamous Pass 'Em. She's one of the first horses I ever bought. She's retired now, but she more than paid for her share of the ranch. For economic reasons, most owners sell unproductive animals, but I can't do it. It seems disloyal somehow."

Despite his single-minded pursuit of work, Noelle could see that money was not Brody's primary motivation. He was driven by the simple desire to be the best at what he did, which just happened to be something he loved very much. She was glad she'd had the chance to see Brody on his own turf. She felt closer to him now that she understood what an integral part of his life his work was.

Hand in hand they strolled toward the house and after making sure the twins were still safely occupied, they walked around the grounds.

"I notice you have a tortoise painted over your barn door," Noelle observed. "Isn't that a strange logo for a man who makes his living with fast horses."

Brody chuckled. "The tortoise thing started a long time ago. I'd just gotten my trainer's license and we took five head down to a track in Texas. Just before the first race, I discovered I'd forgotten to pack the blinders. So I sent Billy to find the tack wagon and he came back with the only pair to be had. As you can guess, they had tortoises on them.

"That seemed like bad luck to me, but Billy convinced me that in Cherokee lore the tortoise had a whole different meaning. We used them and four of our horses won that day. Ever since then, tortoises have been my thing."

"So you're superstitious?"

"No more than any other horseman. For instance, I wouldn't think of tossing a hat on a bed. But unlike some pro athletes I've heard of, I don't wear the same pair of socks to every race."

"I'm relieved to hear that," Noelle said as she wrinkled her nose.

"I'd show you my office, but it's a mess right now. I can't seem to keep up with the paper work anymore. I have an accounting firm to handle the yearly stuff, but bookkeeping entries have to be made every day and I'm way behind," he admitted.

She felt a twinge of guilt for all the time he spent with her. "Maybe I could help you?" she suggested.

He looked at her and smiled. "Maybe you could at that. I'd almost forgotten you work in a bank. I won't make you start today, but I'll show you the office."

She followed him up a stairway outside the barn to the loft above. "It's up here," he told her. "When paper started taking over the house, I converted the loft." At the top of the stairs was a small deck which provided an unemcumbered view of the surrounding farm.

"You must feel like the lord of the manor when you're up here surveying your lands," she teased.

He looked out past the barns to the rolling fields beyond. "I'll admit to a fair amount of pride. When I think where Riley and I came from, it's hard to believe this is all ours. Owning this place is the security we never had. Maybe that's why it's so important to me."

Noelle placed her hand on his arm. "It's beautiful here, you have a right to be proud. I could get used to this place real easy," she said wistfully without thinking how her words might be interpreted.

Brody squeezed her hand. The significance was not lost on him. "Maybe if I spent less time patting myself on the back and more time on the blasted books, I wouldn't be in such a mess." He unlocked the door and gestured for her to go in first.

The office ran the entire length of the barn. Along one wall, above two cluttered desks, were framed pictures of the ranch in both its early stages and as it appeared now. The other long wall consisted of a glass-enclosed trophy case full of ribbons and trophies and silver cups from past Futurities and derbies.

Framed photos of Brody with the flower-bedecked winners were scattered among them and Noelle had a chance to see how he'd looked as a very young man.

"This is where I end up sleeping half the time," he told her as he walked to the far end of the room where a pit grouping of overstuffed furniture showed signs of heavy use. "There's a small bathroom in there and those folding doors hide a kitchenette."

"I have to tell you, Brody, I'm impressed. To think I fed you burgers and entertained you with putt putt golf, while all the time you were this . . . this horse mogul."

He laughed. "Hardly that. Yet."

She peered in the case at the many trophies. "Don't be so modest. These speak of your accomplishments."

"I can't take all the credit. Riley and I are a team. He may not be up to snuff right now, but he's got good instincts where horses are concerned. Unfortunately, his instincts about women aren't as infallible. But I think he may be improving because I sure like Darcy Durant. She just might be the one to straighten him out."

"Riley has hurt Darcy too much," Noelle told him. "I don't think she's interested in the job."

"I don't blame her. He can be a hardheaded sonofagun sometimes. When he gets back from whatever tear he's on, I have a few words for him."

"Don't be too hard on him, Brody, you're all he has."

"I know," he answered, the resignation in his voice telling her just how big that responsibility was. "But right now, pretty lady, I have a few words for you."

"Oh?"

He grabbed her and fell back on the sofa, settling her on top of him. He was desperate with wanting, crazy to discover all the secrets of her body. But most of all he wanted to forget the outside world and lose himself in the wonder of her. He felt his heart thump crazily beneath the hand she splayed on his chest and wondered how he could begin to tell her what she'd come to mean to him.

Or should he? How could he ask her to share his frantic life-style when she wanted and needed the security of predictability? Would she even be willing to try to adjust to a life that revolved around racetracks? Could she learn to love him, only to do without him three-quarters of the time?

As he pulled her close and found her lips with his, those questions didn't seem important.

What mattered was the way they made each other feel. She was real and warm and loving. She gave him a sense of family and future. She was stability and someone to come home to after another season of dreams. She was the woman he'd never thought to find.

The melding of their lips and eager communication of their bodies created a transfusion of emotion unlike any Noelle had ever known. She wanted to give herself in the fullest sense of the word. She'd give Brody anything, everything. Bare every secret, share every hope. If only he could need her as much as she needed him.

"Noelle, there's something I have to say." Unsure of how to proceed, he decided to wing it. The way he had that first day at the zoo.

But he didn't get a chance to do even that. The ringing phone shattered the moment.

"Jeez, perfect timing," he grumbled as he got up to answer it. He perched on the edge of the desk and picked up the receiver. "Sawyer," he barked.

Noelle watched as his expression changed from irritated to furious. "Damn it, Riley! People have been worried about you. Don't you ever think of anyone but yourself? Where the hell are you, anyway?"

He listened quietly for a moment and then a look of astonishment crossed his face. "You're where?"

Noelle imagined all the things that could have happened to Riley—maybe he was hurt, in the hospital.

Brody raked his hand through his hair in a familiar gesture. "For God's sake, Riley, do you know what kind of position you're putting me in here? All right. Dammit, I said all right. Sit tight, I'm coming."

He slammed down the handset. "Riley's in jail."

"In jail? For what?"

"A misdemeanor, thank God. Drunk and disorderly."

"Where?"

"In Sand Springs. He rode up there with some good ol' boys he met in a bar. It's a three hour drive, but I have to go and bail him out."

"I understand." Noelle hated herself for begrudging Riley the time he'd get to spend with Brody, but this was supposed to be her day. She wouldn't see him until after Labor Day and now they wouldn't even have a chance to say goodbye properly.

He returned to the sofa and gathered her into his arms. "I'm sorry about today. I wanted it to be special."

"It has been," she assured him.

"You don't understand. I had big plans. It wasn't supposed to end this way."

"Maybe it's best. If things had been much more 'special,'" she said suggestively, "they might have gotten out of hand."

He kissed her deeply. "That's exactly what I had in mind."

She sighed. Despite the kisses, despite the longing, despite the heart-breaking ache he made her feel, something else always came first with him. It wasn't his fault but neither was it hers. It was a terrible thought, but maybe they weren't meant to be. "Shouldn't you get started?"

He stood in the middle of the room, his mind outlining what he had to do. "I'll have to cancel my flight to Ruidoso, arrange for a rental car to drive to Sand Springs, and fly out of Tulsa tomorrow."

"I'll do that for you while you pack," she offered.

He kissed her again, this time appreciatively. "Thanks, I need a good woman."

"Or a good bookkeeper," she retorted as she danced away from him. She sobered when she realized that in a few more minutes he'd be gone.

He locked the door. "How would I get along without you?"

"The way you always do," she said softly as she trailed him down the stairs.

As they crossed the yard she noticed Dusty and Danny climbing trees with their new friends.

"No more climbing," she warned. "Those trees are much too big."

"But, Momma, it's my turn to be the sheriff and I gotta catch the bad guys," Danny grumbled.

"You can chase bad guys on the ground," she pointed out in her firmest mother voice.

"Aw heck," Dusty complained as he holstered his toy gun and ran after the other boys.

"You're a hard woman, Mrs. Chandler," Brody teased.

"Being a mother is hard work," she reminded him.

Later, they walked to his truck together but Brody was reluctant to leave. "You do understand why I have to go, don't you?"

"Yes. Go now. I'll gather up the boys in a few minutes and say goodbye to Billy and Wanda." She pulled his head down to hers and watched his eyes close, his lips part in anticipation.

He kissed her gently, brushing her mouth with his in a teasing, tantalizing way. His tongue slid inside her mouth when she moaned with desire. Drawing away, he said, "There's something we have to discuss."

"There's a lot of things we need to discuss, but I don't think this is time."

A blood-chilling cry suddenly shattered the peaceful morning. Brody and Noelle turned as one and sprinted to the trees where the boys had been playing. Danny lay crumpled in the grass beneath it, sobbing and screaming.

"What happened, Dusty?" Noelle's heart had started hammering at the first cry and she'd fully expected to find her child unconscious. His hysterical weeping actually relieved her as she bent over him checking for injuries.

Dusty looked up and promptly burst into tears. "We was playing sheriff... and Danny fell... I shot him out of the tree."

Tommy and Terry stood by anxiously. "It was an accident, Brody. Dusty didn't mean to really hurt him."

"I know." Brody gently turned Danny over and the child cried out in pain. "M-m-my arm hurts," he sobbed.

Two inches above the impossibly tiny wrist, the straight line of the ulna was interrupted by a large notch.

"It's broken," Brody said needlessly as he felt the fractured bone. Turning to Tommy and Terry he said, "Why don't you boys run to the house and get me a pillow. We need something to rest Danny's arm on while we drive to the hospital."

They hurried to do his bidding and were back in just a few minutes. By that time, Billy and Wanda had come out to see if they could help.

Danny cried out again as Brody lifted him into his arms. "Let's take him to Children's, it's closest."

Once they had the child settled as comfortably as they could in his car seat, Noelle turned to Brody. "I'll take him. You have to go to Sand Springs, remember?"

Brody was shocked by her suggestion. "That can wait. I want to make sure Danny's okay. Don't you want me to come?"

"Only if you want to. Follow in your truck and you can leave from the hospital." Noelle noticed the pain her curt words caused, but she was too worried about her son to care.

During the tense drive to the hospital, she soothed the scared boys by maintaining a motherly calm. She kept telling herself that from the moment children were born, their mothers had to prepare for mishaps like this. They were all too common in childhood and a required part of motherhood training.

But that knowledge did not make the long drive any easier. Nor did Danny's sobbing and Dusty's frantic apologies. Her own guilt was magnified by the fact that the accident had occurred while her attention was focused on Brody. It had been wrong to relax her vigilance, even to be alone with him.

She should have found comfort in knowing Brody would be with her at the hospital. But it wasn't forthcoming. She'd been ready to give him anything he wanted, but today she'd discovered that she was still at the bottom of his list of priorities. If Danny had waited five more minutes before falling, Brody would have been on his way to Sand Springs. Or to Ruidoso. Or a hundred other places that were more important to him than home.

After seeing Cimarron Noelle couldn't understand why he would exchange the lovely house and quiet setting for impersonal motel rooms. Was it because of his past? Did he feel like a stranger in the house he built because for so long he hadn't really belonged anywhere?

She'd probably never know. Whatever problems Brody had, he wasn't willing to share with her. So he would have to solve them himself. And in the meantime, she'd be a fool to rely on him, to count on him being there when she needed him.

Once they were admitted through the emergency room, Brody and Dusty were left to cool their heels in the waiting area. Down the hall Danny's screams died down for a few minutes and then rose to wall-shaking proportions. After a few more wails, he was silent.

"It sure is quiet now, ain't it, Brody?" Dusty asked nervously. "Danny didn't die, did he?"

The face that looked up at Brody was dirty and tear-streaked. It totally wrenched his heart. He pulled the child onto his lap and hugged him tight. "No, of course not. They probably gave him some medicine for the pain and it stopped hurting."

"I bet we're gonna get in trouble for climbing that tree, ain't we?"

"What do you think?"

Dusty stared at the tips of his little tennis shoes. "I say yes."

The receptionist gave Dusty some paper and crayons and he was busy drawing his brother a picture when Noelle came out into the waiting room.

Brody jumped up. "Is he all right?"

"He's asleep right now. They gave him an injection for the pain. The doctor just showed me the X-rays. It's a clean fracture so it should heal quickly."

She explained that when the orthopedist on call got around to Danny, he'd set the bone and wrap it in a temporary cast until the swelling subsided. In a week or so, he'd put on the plaster cast.

"It's been over an hour," Brody said anxiously. "Do you mean to tell me the bone doctor hasn't even seen him yet?"

The pressure of the past two hours made Noelle snap. "This is a busy hospital. Danny wasn't the only child who got hurt today." In the cubicle next to Danny's, doctors had worked futilely over a tiny car crash victim and she thought of how fragile a young life really was. Her place was with her children who needed her, not with this man who did not.

"If you're in a hurry, Brody, just go on. I'm sure I can handle it from here."

He saw immediately that she'd misunderstood. "I'm not worried about leaving. I was thinking about Danny lying in there waiting."

"Is that why you've looked at the clock half a dozen times in the past five minutes?" She kept her voice low, but her feelings ran high.

"Noelle," he pleaded.

"Riley's your brother, so go to him. Blood's thicker than water, and all that."

"Noelle, why are you doing this?" Brody didn't understand her excess of emotions. His remark had been innocent enough. And he was just as worried about Danny as she was.

"Just go on." She felt dangerously close to tears.

She was shutting him out and Brody had no idea what he'd done wrong. "Are you blaming me for what happened? Is that it? Believe me, I feel guilty. If I hadn't taken them to Frontier City, they wouldn't have tried to reenact that shoot-out."

"It was an accident and nobody's fault."

He reached out to her, but she moved away from him. "Something's wrong. I can feel it. I know I should have kept a closer eye on them, or been there to catch him when he fell. But I'm not a parent. I have a lot to learn."

"The boys are my responsibility, not yours. If anyone should feel guilty, it's me. I can't always protect them from the consequences of their actions, but neither can I expect them to always use good judgment. They're not adults."

"What's that mean?" he asked.

"It means that just as little boys must climb trees, so must men make their own decisions. In order to grow, they have to try and perhaps fail, but they have to learn from their own experiences. In the end the choice is theirs, all we can do is teach them the hazards of taking risks."

"Noelle—"

"You've never given Riley that choice."

Brody raked his hand through his hair again. "I thought we were talking about Danny. How did Riley get into this?"

"You use your brother as an excuse not to love anyone else. You seem to think that love is some finite thing that must be carefully doled out. You smother Riley and you don't have anything left for others."

Brody was completely unprepared for this conversation. Earlier this morning he'd been ready to tell her just how much he had come to love her and the boys. He'd wanted her to help him figure out how to juggle all his responsibilities successfully. But her words were so damning, her voice so unforgiving, that he could say nothing.

"I see I made my point." She turned to Dusty, but he was too busy coloring to notice the adults.

"Noelle, whether you realize it or not, you and the boys are important to me. Don't leave."

"As I recall, you're the one who's always leaving." The words were hard to say, but that didn't make them any less necessary. "I think I finally figured out what's been wrong between us. You're satisfied with the way your life is and there's no place in it for me."

"That's not true," he protested.

Noelle wanted to believe him, but now that she knew why Brody's work was so important to him, she could never ask him to give it up. "I don't care to place or show, Brody. I won't settle for less than first place in your life. I'm sorry if that sounds selfish, but it's how I feel."

He felt her slipping away from him, but he didn't know what to say. She was right. She deserved to come first in all things. He just couldn't give her that right now. Maybe he needed the time in Ruidoso. Maybe if he threw himself into getting ready for the race, he could figure out what to do.

"Go to Riley, Brody. Go to your horses. That's what you want." It was better to send him away than to try and cut him up in little pieces that would be no good to anyone.

He stood and turned his hat in his hands. "I don't know what I want to do anymore."

"You made your decision a long time ago." She couldn't meet his pain-filled gaze and battled the urge to hold him and soothe him as she had Danny. "Go."

He wanted to stay, he wanted to take her in his arms and never let her go. But he had to. She didn't want or need the pitiful little he could offer her. "Can I say goodbye to Danny?"

"He's still asleep. I'll tell him you said goodbye."

Brody turned to Dusty who had finished the crayon picture. "I guess this is adios, pardner," he told the boy.

"I hope your horses all win, Brody. Here." Dusty thrust the paper into Brody's hands. "I was making this for Danny, but you take it. I'll make him another one."

Brody's throat tightened. "Thanks, buddy. I'll take it to New Mexico with me."

Without realizing what he was doing, Brody leaned toward Noelle. "I'll see you when I get back?" It was a question he was afraid to ask.

"I don't think that's a good idea, Brody. This is going to be hard for all concerned. Especially the boys. Somehow I think losing you is going to have a bigger effect on them than losing their father."

"We can work something out, can't we?"

"No." Noelle was shaking, but she spoke firmly. "I know how much you hate to commit yourself, but will you promise me one thing?"

"Just tell me," he replied quickly. Willing, now that it was too late, to promise her anything.

"Don't try to see us and don't call. Under the circumstances, I think a clean break is best."

"Noelle, you can't mean that."

"You can promise that much, can't you?" she whispered desperately as her eyes filled with the tears she didn't want him to see.

"I promise." He just wasn't sure he could keep it. "I don't want us to end like this."

"And I can't keep doing the goodbye scene until we get it the way you want it."

"I meant . . ."

"Goodbye, Brody."

He turned without another word and as the automatic doors swooshed open, she said his name softly. "Brody?"

He whirled around. "Yes?" He'd never known such a small word could harbor so much hope.

"Don't bet on any more long shots." Noelle picked up Dusty and headed down the hall to Danny. She had to hurry before the bitter tears fell. She had to hurry before she ran crying after him.

Chapter Twelve

I guess we both lost our cowboys," Darcy commiserated.

"Easy come, easy go." Noelle's agreement caused a catch in her voice.

"If that's true, why's the going always so hard?" Darcy's question was rhetorical. She'd already told Noelle about her plans and they'd had a good cry over them. This might be the last such talk they had for a while and they were determined to make the most of it.

The two friends sat in Noelle's living room, a bottle of Evian mineral water between them. The hour was late, the house quiet. Gershwin's "Rhapsody in Blue," a fitting accompaniment to the mood of the evening, swelled from the stereo.

Darcy had been waiting with a big bag of fast food hamburgers when Noelle arrived home from the hospital. They'd fed the twins and put them to bed early. Danny succumbed quickly to the effects of the Demerol he'd received at the hospital and Dusty was worn out from the events of the long day.

The women had already discussed the Sawyer brothers at length and were now emotionally wrung out. "I wish you weren't going," Noelle told Darcy.

"Don't start talking like that, or I'll chicken out. I never would have gotten up the courage in the first place if Mom hadn't insisted."

"Are you sure she'll be all right with you in Nashville?"

"Cord will take care of her. And Aunt Bertie's moving in next week. She's a widow, too. They'll be good company for each other."

Noelle eyed her friend appraisingly. "You've talked about taking risks and finding yourself and making it big with your singing, but it's time to tell the truth. You're doing this because of Riley, aren't you?"

She nodded. "When Riley walked out on me that morning, after all we'd shared the night before, I knew I'd have to leave or go crazy. When I talked to Mom, she urged me to go to Nashville."

"Knowing how close you two are, that must have been hard for her."

Darcy tucked her bare feet close to her body and hugged her knees. "It nearly broke my heart when she started crying and talking about Daddy. You see, alcoholism doesn't just hurt the addict. She likes Riley, but she wants to spare me what she suffered."

Noelle patted her friend's shoulder. "I understand why you're going. It's just that I'll miss you so much." She felt the tears coming again and blinked them back. It seemed like she'd been crying for hours. First about Brody and then about Darcy and Riley.

When she told her friend about the scene at the hospital, Darcy tried to comfort her. "Brody and Riley are alike in a lot of ways. I have to think it's because of what they went through as kids. Riley uses alcohol to cope and ease the pain, and Brody uses work. Different dependency, same effect."

Noelle knew Darcy was right. She already missed Brody but she felt she'd done the right thing. "I guess it'll take something bigger than us to make them realize how self-destructive they are."

They talked until nearly 2:00 a.m. About the good times, the bad times and every time in between. After Darcy left, Noelle got ready for bed. She was drained but she felt better. It was as though talking about Brody had somehow started the healing process. Started, maybe, but it would a long time before she stopped thinking about him.

Even longer before she stopped loving him.

She saw Darcy off to Nashville the following Saturday, two days before Labor Day and the big race. Goodbyes were tearful, but Darcy promised to call as soon as she found a place and settled in.

Noelle, who was in no shape to work, took her two-week vacation early to be at home with Danny. There wouldn't be any trips to the lake this summer. Some of the money in the vacation jar could be spent on special treats and entertainment for the boys, and the rest would go toward the insurance deductible. She'd never imagined such a small bone would cost so much to repair.

Brody had kept his promise. He hadn't called. Glory Roberts stopped by one day, loaded down with picture books and toy horses, ostensibly to check on Danny and say hello.

Noelle assumed the visit was at Brody's behest because before she left Glory said, "I know this is none of my business, but what the heck? I've always been accused of being a buttinsky. Are you and Brody really kaput?"

"That's an interesting way to put it, but yes."

"We're all worried about him. Pap called to see how things were shaping up for the race and he said Brody sounded kind of out of it. I think he's hurting bad. It's not like my big brother to let anything get in his way of winning."

"I'm sorry to hear that," Noelle said softly. "I know how much winning means to him."

"It doesn't mean half as much to him as you and those two little boys in there," Glory told her.

"I disagree. But even if you are right, it only makes things more impossible."

"Try to understand, Noelle. I was very young when Brody and Riley came to live with us. To me Brody seemed so grown-up. He never cried or showed his feelings, never acted like a kid at all. He worked more than anyone expected him to and he shied away from attention."

"He certainly isn't shy now," Noelle put in.

"No. He isn't. If anything, he overcompensates."

"Brody's the most self-sufficient person I've ever met."

"Oh, no! That's where you're wrong, Noelle. Brody has needs, he's just adept at denying them. One night about a month after he came to live with us, I heard him crying in his room when he thought everyone was asleep. Being a little busybody, totally lacking in sensitivity and scruples, I barged in and demanded to know what was wrong.

"Didn't he like living with us, I asked him. Didn't he like me and Mama and Pap? Was he unhappy about the food? What? He was ten or eleven at the time and thought he was too big to be caught crying, so he toughened right up, put back on the mask. He told me he liked us plenty, that was the problem. We were too good to him and sooner or later we'd realize we were wasting our time with such a good-for-nothing."

"How could any child, even one with Brody's background, think so little of himself?" Noelle asked.

"It's disturbing, isn't it? I was just a kid, so I said that was the dumbest thing I'd ever heard. He started crying again and all of a sudden he was talking. Really talking, for the first time. He said his father had told him he'd always be a loser and would never amount to anything."

"And Brody's still trying to prove him wrong? Even now, after all his success?"

"I think so."

"And when I wouldn't accept what he had to offer, I just reinforced all those old insecurities."

"That's how I see it. He doesn't think he's good enough for you. But Brody's got a lot to offer a woman, he just doesn't realize it. I was hoping you did."

Glory walked to the door. "He wouldn't appreciate me coming here like this, but I did it because you two shouldn't let anything stand between you."

Noelle thought about Glory's revelations for the next three days. On Labor Day she took the boys on a picnic to Lake Hefner. Danny had adjusted easily to his injury and romped and played on the grass as if nothing had happened. Only when Danny wanted a little special attention did he use his arm to his advantage.

The twins talked about Brody as much as usual and Noelle wondered how she was going to tell them that the man they loved so much was no longer a part of their lives. They assumed he'd be back when the race was over, and she didn't have the courage to tell them otherwise.

Soon they got tired of sliding and flopped down on the blanket beside her. She stroked back the silky hair plastered to their hot foreheads.

"Today's somethin' 'portant, idn't it?" Dusty asked.

"It's Labor Day. A day set aside in recognition of working people," she explained.

"I don't mean that. I mean Brody's race."

"Yes, today is something special for Brody."

"I'll be glad when he gets back," Danny said.

Noelle tried to find the words to tell her sons that they wouldn't be seeing their hero again. "Brody's very busy now."

"We know."

"He might not have time to come and see us like he used to."

Dusty watched a small black beetle creep across the blanket with the intensity only a child could lavish on such an insignificant part of nature. "He'll come. That's what's so good about Brody. He's...he's..." He grappled with his limited vocabulary for the right word. "He's 'pendable."

"Yeah," Danny put in. "Even when's he gone, we know he's thinkin' about us, pickin' out presents and plannin' stuff. It don't matter how much he has to go away, 'cause he makes coming back so great."

Noelle felt the sting of tears. She hugged her sons close and kissed them loudly. "How'd you two get so wise in only four years?"

"Cause we have a smart mother?" Dusty suggested with a sly look as he sneaked into the basket for another cookie.

She shook her head. "I don't think I'm so smart."

"Sure you are, Momma. Mrs. Johnson says being smart ain't what you know," Danny explained patiently.

"Being smart," Dusty finished for him, "is what you do with what you know."

The tears came then, but for the first time in a week, Noelle wasn't sad. She'd been wrong and her children were right. Brody was dependable, he took promises seriously. He'd never be like Steve.

His homecomings made all the leave-takings meaningless. Why hadn't she realized it before? It had taken the innocent wisdom of four-year-olds to show her that going away didn't matter. What mattered was always coming home.

She'd played second fiddle to Steve's dream because they had come first in his heart. That rejection had made her afraid that horse training would always be Brody's first love. Maybe it was, but it didn't have to be his only love.

She started gathering up the picnic things. "Thank you, boys, and tell your teacher I thank her, too."

"Do we have to leave now?"

"Yes. We want to get home in time to watch the race on TV, don't we?"

She sat nervously throughout the prerace program. When the field was announced, she was pleased to see that two of Brody's horses had qualified to run; Finnegan's Fancy and the early favorite, Overnight Sensation.

Overnight Sensation had won seven out of ten races for the year and was the stand-out entry in an otherwise evenly matched field. The four-forty sprint down the Ruidoso Downs straightaway would be worth a cool million to the winner. The trainer's share would be ten percent.

But the payoff for Brody would come in more than dollars and cents. Noelle knew how much a victory this year meant to him and as post time neared she found the tension almost unbearable.

The television camera panned to a shot of Brody talking to an interviewer. Noelle sat up straighter and punched up the volume. She listened as he discussed qualifying times and described Overnight's special qualities. She wasn't paying much attention to what he said. All she could think of was how tired he looked and how fast his television smile faded when he thought he was off camera.

She'd already made up her mind to call him. She had to explain why she'd reacted like she had that day at the hospital. She owed him an apology and she hoped he'd offer her another chance. If he did, she was sure she could give him enough love to heal all those old wounds.

Despite Overnight Sensation's easy victory in the All-American Futurity, Brody didn't feel much like celebrating that night. Today had been the culmination of months of intense work. For this race alone he had logged over five thousand air miles. Winning had been his one and only goal. It meant everything.

But it meant nothing without Noelle.

He walked into his motel room and threw his hat on the desk. It had taken hours to get away from all the well-wishers at the track, the reporters, the sportscasters, the fans. Overnight's owner was on cloud nine and he'd invited Brody to a big wingding at his hotel. He could hardly say no, but he'd slipped away at the first opportunity.

He just didn't feel like partying. He sat on the bed and spotted Dusty's drawing propped on the bedside table. The inexpertly rendered horses and smiling stick figures made him homesick.

But if he went home, would Noelle and the boys be there? He stared at the telephone, wondering if he should break his promise and call her. Since nothing had changed, what could he say?

During the past week he'd considered all possible scenarios. He could give up training, but he didn't know anything else and they'd all starve. He could try to get a nine-to-five job, but his own cluttered desk proved that he had no inclination or talent for paperwork. He could sell out to Riley and putter around in the flower beds with Bobber Smith while Noelle brought home the bacon, but he'd soon grow to hate himself for that.

A soft tap on the door interrupted his thoughts. When he opened it, Riley was standing there.

"Hey, big brother," he joshed. "You don't look much like the conquering hero."

Brody flopped back down on the bed. "Don't feel like one, either."

"I saw you sneaking away from Lehman's party and I wondered if you had time to talk to me."

"Sure, Riley. I always have time for you."

He sat on the other bed. "I know. That's one of your main problems. When I called you that day from jail, why didn't you tell me to rot and good riddance?"

Brody, preoccupied with his own thoughts, looked up sharply. "What are you talking about?"

"When you got there, you didn't say a word. You cleaned up my mess, paid my bills and put me on the plane with you. You didn't yell at me or cuss me or tell me what a worthless pain in the butt I was."

"I couldn't. That's what Joe would have done." And Brody wasn't like Joe. He would never be like Joe.

Riley slumped. "No, Brody. That's what I deserved. In case you haven't noticed, I *am* a pain in the butt. I'm also a drunk."

"You drink, yes," Brody concurred. "But you're not a drunk. Joe was a drunk."

"And I'm heading down the same road. Darcy Durant was the best thing that ever happened to me and she'll never speak to me again. Do you want to know why?"

"Do you want to tell me?" Brody had been careful not to pry too deeply into the motives behind Riley's sudden disappearance and subsequent arrest. He'd hoped that if they didn't talk about it, it wouldn't happen again.

"God knows why, but Darcy loved me. I know I love her. She pointed out that I was throwing my life away and asked me to marry her. She said she'd help me get straight. She knows all about it because her father was an alcoholic. She joined Al-Anon when she was eight years old. She was willing to risk everything for me."

"So what were you doing in a drunk tank in Sand Springs, Oklahoma?" Brody wanted to know.

"Hiding. From Darcy, from myself, from you. In a way, I think I was still hiding from Joe."

"Riley—"

"No, listen to me, Brody, because this concerns you. I know I let you down. I let Dub and Ruby down. I let Candi's kids down. I let Darcy down. Hell, I was well on my way to making a career out of hurting people. But as of now, that's going to change."

"How?"

"I've made an appointment at a rehab center in Dallas. I'm leaving in the morning. I'll be out of touch for a while but when I get back, you can be proud of me."

Brody hugged his brother and was reminded of all the times he'd made Riley's problems his own. Of all the times he'd stood between Riley and the world. No more. Riley was ready to stand on his own now.

"I'm already proud of you, little brother. I always have been." Brody didn't try to fight the strong emotions he felt and if his eyes filled with tears, so be it.

Riley clapped Brody on the back and sat up. "Now that I've got you in such a good mood, I have a big favor to ask you."

"You always were a manipulating little twerp."

"You remember the sixth race today? The twenty-five hundred dollar claiming race?"

"Yeah, what about it?"

"I claimed the winner, Rebel's Redemption. Not a bad name for a horse that's going to redeem it's owner, huh? I'd like you to take him back to Cimarron for me and start training him while I'm gone. I know it's a lot to ask, but I plan to make you a fifty-fifty partner in him."

"You don't have to do that." Brody could tell by the conviction in Riley's voice and the look of confidence on his face that Rebel's Redemption would be the project that would give his brother back his self-respect.

"Too late. I've already put your name on the papers." When Brody grinned Riley said, "You don't get off that easy. There's something else."

"I was afraid of that."

"Go home and do whatever you have to do to get Noelle back. She's a good woman and you need each other. Tell her that when I get my act cleaned up, I'm going to do more of the traveling, so you don't have to. Tell her I'll start carrying my share again."

Brody hugged his brother. He was grinning and making plans and trying to think of the words he'd need for Noelle.

"And Brody? If you talk to Darcy, tell her not to give up on me. I tried to call her myself, but her brother said she moved to Nashville last week and he wouldn't give me her number. I don't blame him. The shape I was in the last time he saw me, I wouldn't give me her number, either."

"I'm sorry about Darcy."

"Me, too. But because of her, I finally found the strength to get it right. Once I make everything up to you, I'm going to make it up to her. I'll win her back."

"Just get well. That's all you have to do for me."

Brody rang Noelle's doorbell even though her little car wasn't in the drive. He had come straight from the airport and hadn't wanted to risk calling. She might not be willing to listen. Maybe in person, she'd hear him out.

"Are you looking for Noelle?" Mrs. Sterling was watering peonies in the yard next door.

"Yes, I am. I just got back into town and was hoping I could catch her."

She was full of information. "Oh, you just missed her. She and the children left for the zoo a few minutes ago."

Brody tipped his hat politely and thanked her before pointing his truck toward the zoo. He only pushed the speed limit a couple of times.

Dusty and Danny were enjoying the gorillas as usual, but Noelle couldn't smile at their antics. They reminded her too much of the last time she'd been here—the day she'd met Brody. But the boys had begged to come and she'd agreed because they'd been so good she hated to deny them such a small pleasure.

Noelle had tried to call Brody at the motel where he usually stayed in Ruidoso, but the clerk had informed her that he'd already checked out. She then called Cimarron and Wanda told her she hadn't heard from him. During the past week, picturing him in one setting or the other had helped her over the rough spots. Not knowing where he was, she felt lost.

Sensing someone watching her, Noelle looked up and saw Brody standing a few feet away, his hat in his hand. His eyes, filled with hope and questions, searched hers.

She closed her eyes and thanked God for sending him home again. When she opened them she felt as if a week of pain had just fell away. She took the first step toward him and he welcomed her into his arms.

Dusty and Danny saw him then and jumped up and down, calling his name, hugging his legs.

"Brody, I'm sorry," she said at the same moment he said, "Noelle, I'm sorry."

"No," she protested. "I never should have—"

"Never say never," he told her before he captured her lips with his. His kiss was an urgent declaration of his feelings and she lost herself in his special magic.

"Congratulations on Overnight Sensation. I'm so happy you won."

"I won a lot more than a race in Ruidoso. I'll tell you all about that later. But now, I want to ask you if you can forgive me."

"For what?"

"For breaking my promise. I know I agreed not to call you or see you, but I couldn't bear it. Love may be a long shot, Noelle, but it's better than no shot at all."

"Long shots sometimes pay off big," she reminded him with a kiss before the twins' excited voices interrupted her.

"Ah, heck, Brody. Stop kissin' Momma and tell us what you bringed us," Dusty fussed.

"This trip I brought your momma something instead." He fished into his pocket and withdrew a black velvet jeweler's case. "I took the liberty of bringing this along. I thought if you agreed to marry me, I could put it on your finger before you changed your mind."

He took the exquisitely cut diamond ring out of its box and held it nervously. "I love you Noelle. I missed you so much this week, I'll do anything to be the man you need me to be."

She took his face tenderly between her hands. "You already are, cowboy. You always have been, I was just too blind to realize it. I love you."

"So maybe that long shot might turn out to be a sure thing?"

She dashed away tears, this time of happiness. "I'd bet on it."

"It won't be easy, but we'll make a fine team, you wait and see. I'll be a good husband and father. I'll stay home more and I won't work so much. When I do travel you can be sure that I'll always come home to you and—"

"Brody," she interrupted with a teasing smile. "Are you sure you're not just trying to get a free bookkeeper?"

"I don't need a bookkeeper. I need the woman I love."

"And I'm that woman?" she asked breathlessly.

"The one and only, for ever and always."

She didn't care that a crowd of strangers were watching the tender declarations. She kissed him with the fervor of a love that would only improve as the years went by.

"So will you? Marry me, I mean?"

"Say yes, Momma," the boys cried. "Say yes."

"Yes, Brody. I'll marry you."

"Yippee!" That shout came from Brody, as well as the boys. "The reason I worked so many hours," he told her, "was because my life was so empty. You and the boys are precious to me and you'll always come first, before all others. We'll solve all the problems because our love is stronger than any of them." And then he added solemnly, "I promise."

Noelle and Brody kissed again to seal that vow, then clasped their little boys hands between them. They thought of home and were caught up in another promise.

A lifetime in the winner's circle.

*   *   *   *   *

COMING NEXT MONTH

#730 BORROWED BABY—Marie Ferrarella
A Diamond Jubilee Book!
Stuck with a six-month-old bundle of joy, reserved policeman Griff Foster became a petrified parent. Then bubbly Liz MacDougall taught him a thing or two about diapers, teething, lullabies and love.

#731 FULL BLOOM—Karen Leabo
When free-spirited Hilary McShane returned early from her vacation, she hadn't expected to find methodical Matthew Burke as a substitute house-sitter. Their life-styles and attitudes clashed, but their love kept growing....

#732 THAT MAN NEXT DOOR—Judith Bowen
New dairy owner Caitlin Forrest was entranced by friendly neighbor Ben Wade. When she discovered that he wanted her farm, however, she wondered exactly how much business he was mixing with pleasure.

#733 HOME FIRES BURNING BRIGHT—Laurie Paige
Book II of HOMEWARD BOUND DUO
Carson McCumber felt he had nothing to offer a woman—especially privileged Tess Garrick. Out to prove the rugged rancher wrong, Tess was determined to keep all the home fires burning....

#734 BETTER TO HAVE LOVED—Linda Varner
Convinced she'd lose, loner Allison Kendall had vowed never to play the game of love. But martial-arts enthusiast Meade Duran was an expert at tearing down all kinds of defenses.

#735 VENUS de MOLLY—Peggy Webb
Cool, controlled banker Samuel Adams became hot under the collar when he thought about his mother marrying Molly Rakestraw's father. But that was before he met the irrepressible Molly!

AVAILABLE THIS MONTH:

Diamond Jubilee Collection

It's our 10th Anniversary... and *you* get a present!

This collection of early Silhouette Romances features novels written by three of your favorite authors:

ANN MAJOR—*Wild Lady*
ANNETTE BROADRICK—*Circumstantial Evidence*
DIXIE BROWNING—*Island on the Hill*

* **These Silhouette Romance titles were first published in the early 1980s and have not been available since!**

* **Beautiful Collector's Edition bound in antique green simulated leather to last a lifetime!**

* **Embossed in gold on the cover and spine!**

✂ **PROOF OF PURCHASE**
